BODY ON THE ESTATE

A gripping murder mystery

DIANE M. DICKSON

Published by The Book Folks

London, 2023

© Diane Dickson

ISBN 978-1-80462-098-4

www.thebookfolks.com

BODY ON THE ESTATE is the sixth standalone title in the DI Jordan Carr mystery series.

A list of characters can be found at the back of this book.

Chapter 1

DI Jordan Carr put the last of his belongings into a cardboard box. He glanced around the room. It was the middle of the day and not many people were at their desks. It was how he had hoped it would be. He shook hands with a couple of colleagues in the Serious and Organised Crime squad and walked out of St Anne Street Headquarters into a bright September afternoon.

He placed the box into the boot of his car and headed down to Liverpool One where his wife and little boy were waiting. They would have a meal in the pizza restaurant and then a trip on the ferry to enjoy the last of the summer weather. The ferry was Nana Gloria's favourite thing about visits to Merseyside and the thought of her made him smile. Close second on her list of 'must visit' locations were the Beatles statues and the poignant little bronze of Eleanor Rigby.

Nana Gloria had been ill and for a while they'd worried about her, but now she was coming up from London to visit and everything in the world was righting itself. On top of that, he'd decided to move from St Anne Street and back out to a smaller station where he would be involved in what he had come to think of as his sort of crime.

David Griffiths, the DCI who had brought him into the squad had left a door open in case he changed his mind. "Give it a go, Jordan," he'd said, "and if you think you've made a mistake, come back. We can give you six months."

He strode past the Walker Art Gallery and on towards the river. Going back to the policing he enjoyed wasn't a mistake. It might not be as impressive as working with

1

international investigations and multi-force inquiries, but this was the right thing for him to do.

Apart from anything else, he'd be working with Stella May. She was a good mate. He enjoyed being with her and knew she was reliable, funny, brave, and decent. The fact that she was a lottery winner who kept her financial status very quiet, was one of the other things he liked about her. She was genuine and keeping it real, just his sort of person.

Sun sparkled off the river as they boarded the Dazzle Ferry.

"Are we staying on or getting off on the other side?" Penny asked.

"I'm happy just to kick back and enjoy the ride. I feel chilled, relieved, and just a tad excited. Look, Harry's loving the boat." He hugged his little boy who was watching wide-eyed as gulls wheeled overhead and clouds scudded past the waterfront. "Is that okay with you?"

"Yeah. Great. We'll go to the Albert Dock after for a glass of something to celebrate. Oh, that's if you want to?"

"Lovely. Don't worry. That was then and this is now," he said, referring to a past case involving the Albert Dock, the Liver Building, and the Pier Head as well. "It's in the past. Can't let these things stay in your head. You know that though, don't you?"

He wrapped his arm around her and settled back on the seat.

Chapter 2

In Old Roan, Julie Scott was tired, grubby, and dishevelled. They'd been up all night. Her eyes were gritty, and her stomach felt full of acid. The holiday had been great, with boisterous nights and sleepy beach days. It had been just what she'd needed. Unfortunately, the return flight on the cut-price airline was in the early hours of the morning. They had to check out of the hotel the day before. The airport was uncomfortable. They drank too much horrible coffee and ate food they didn't want just to pass the time. Pat said it was always like this, unless you could afford to fly scheduled. She should know, she'd been a lot. She was even recognised in some of the bars and that had added to the fun. Julie had always fancied a trip to Spain, but she hadn't wanted to go on her own. When Pat told her she'd got a special deal, a two-for-one on the flight, it was too good to miss, and it had been great. It had taken her mind off things and now she felt ready to carry on. It was time to make the difficult decisions.

It was strange that she and Pat had clicked. They should have hated each other, but they didn't, and she was turning into a great mate. One thing Julie needed right now was a good friend and it seemed that Pat had turned up at just the right time.

They'd said they'd go again, but she wasn't sure that it would ever happen. Well, they'd see. Other stuff had to happen first and who knew where it would lead.

Dragging her wheelie suitcase up the path, she waved to Mrs Jones, who was peering through the net curtains in the house next door. She was a bit of a curtain twitcher but pleasant enough. Now, though, Julie was going in the shower, cup of tea and then bed.

She unlocked the door and stepped into the hallway, kicking off her shoes. She waited for the feeling of home; the smell of her own place.

It was obvious quickly that something wasn't right. The bowl of potpourri that stood on a cupboard in the hallway was scattered across the carpet. On her way to the kitchen, she crunched over the dried petals and little cones. Tears filled her eyes even before she reached the room. Shards of broken glass and crockery sparkled in the light from the kitchen window. Cupboard doors sagged open, and packets of rice and pasta littered the tiles, telling her all she needed to know. She let go of the suitcase handle and sank onto the hall carpet.

She should be doing something, calling someone, but all she could do right then was moan and sob. Then she found she could swear. A stream of expletives that would have shocked her mother poured out. She cursed the bastards who had invaded her home and made her return to this chaos.

She rested her head against the wall and closed her eyes. There was no way to know how long she might have stayed there if it hadn't been for the creak of the floorboards.

Breath caught in her throat and the hairs on her arms prickled as she scuttered backwards towards the living room. She shuffled into the room and dragged out her mobile phone. As she poked at three nines, she heard footsteps on the stairs. She bobbed down behind the settee as the emergency operator responded.

"Emergency – which service do you need?"

She couldn't speak, could hardly draw in air. Her heart thumped and pounded, and she waited to hear the front door slam as the intruder left. It didn't come, and the operator was insisting on a response. She didn't dare make a sound.

The operator spoke again, urging her to respond with anything, a cough, a whisper or, if that was impossible, to press double five on her keypad. She clicked the buttons. Her call was transferred to the police.

The call handler tried to get her to speak. She tapped her fingernail across the screen. The small noise was acknowledged. They told her to keep her phone switched on and they would trace her. The voice was calm and measured. The noises from the hall were violent. There was a crash as something heavy hit the floor, probably the hat stand, and it was then she remembered her suitcase was still there. It was in the middle of the floor where she had dropped it. Whoever it was out there would know she was in the house. There was nothing to be gained crouching in a terrified heap waiting to be found. She had to move.

She screamed her address into the phone, told them she needed help, that she was in danger. She tore across the room and out into the hall. On the way, she grabbed a glass vase from the sideboard and raised it above her head.

As she spun into the hall, the door smashed back against the wall. Her blood was up. She didn't stop. She sped after the fleeing figure screaming at the top of her voice, haring down the street in her stocking feet screeching obscenities. He was faster than she was. He reached the junction before she did, and by the time she reached the corner, he was nowhere to be seen. She heard a siren and a blue-and-white patrol car slewed to a halt outside her house. Mrs Jones was already on the roadside and pointing to where Julie stood, bewildered and shaking, with a cut-glass vase clutched in her arms.

Chapter 3

Jordan slid into the driving seat of his VW Golf. He waved at Penny who was standing in the doorway with Harry on her hip. His world. She waved, then blew him a kiss and yelled out, "Good luck," waggling Harry's hand up and down, all smiles.

She hid the worry, she always had.

He knew the way to Copy Lane, and when he arrived Stella May was in the car park waiting for him.

"All right, mate?" She gave him a quick hug. "You ready for this? It's ace having you here."

She led him down the corridor to where there was an office set aside for him. "Look at you with your own office," she said as he ran his hand over the desktop leaving a trail in the dust.

Jordan took a breath. "Okay. Let's get this out of the way," he said.

She waited in silence with a good idea of what he was referring to.

"I know you transferred here because there was a chance that you'd get a promotion, among other things. When I put in for a new posting, I didn't think this was where I'd end up."

She shook her head. "I know. It's just the way things have turned out. Who knew DI Silver was on the edge like that? Although it's awful that we didn't realise. Anyway, I haven't put in enough time, I knew they couldn't give it to me. Honest to God, Jordan, it's fine."

"How is he, have you heard?"

"Still in the hossie. It's gonna be a long job, they reckon. Well, mental illness, it's never easy, is it?"

"Poor sod. After twenty years he goes out like this. Were you here?"

"Yeah, but it was weird. He just walked out of his office not speaking to anyone. Left his coat, his phone, everything. It was a while before we realised there was a problem. Anyway, they found him down at the Pier Head just after midnight. He was just staring across the water."

"Do you think he'll be back?"

"Word is it's doubtful. Anyway, listen, mate. I don't hold this against you." She swept a hand around the space. "I like working with you. You've got a lot you can teach me. I can wait for a bit longer."

Jordan smiled and leaned back in the chair which gave an ominous creak. "Well, that's nice, thanks. So, what's happening?"

"Okay, you need to go and see the DCI, obviously. Then we're heading out to Old Roan. Got to see a woman who was robbed yesterday."

"A mugging?"

"No, a break-in. Came back from holiday to find the house ransacked and the vandal still there. He'd run off by the time the patrol turned up, but she was pretty shaken. The DCI wants us to go and have a word, plain clothes and all that. It's all to do with attaching more importance to robberies and street crime. Showing the public that we're learning lessons and taking it more seriously."

"Okay. I have to say I do have some sympathy. It's ghastly being robbed, and finding the scally still in the house must have been horrible for her."

"I guess. Apparently, she hid at first then she chased him, which was pretty brave, if unwise. Anyway, how about a cup of coffee and then we'll get on with it all?"

"Great," he said, "I brought a machine. It's in the car but we can just have a quick one under the circumstances."

Stella grinned at him as she nipped out into the main room, and returned with two takeaway cups. "Not as good as your stuff but better than my instant. There you go."

Jordan popped the top of the cup and poured the drink into the mug he'd brought with him. "Right, fill me in on this woman and her robbery."

Chapter 4

Julie Scott was hunched in front of the flickering flames of a faux log fire. She was dressed in a soft tracksuit and had a blanket around her shoulders.

"I can't get warm," she said.

"Shall I make you a cup of tea?" Stella turned towards the kitchen.

"No, don't. I've drunk tea, coffee, and soup and I'm waterlogged with it."

"I guess it's a bit early for a nip of the hard stuff," Jordan said.

"Oh, I've had that as well, don't worry. Nothing helps. I don't know where to start with this lot." She nodded at a pile of broken ornaments in the corner. "The whole place needs sorting. It feels dirty. I couldn't go to bed last night. Why wreck the place like this? I just don't get it."

"Is there anyone who can help you with it?" Stella asked.

"No, not really. I wouldn't ask any of my mates, it's too manky and upsetting. I would have asked my mam but she's not strong enough nowadays. I haven't told her because she'd go to pieces. I'll get to it. To be honest I feel like throwing it all away. They said not to do anything until they'd done the fingerprints. Have you any idea how long that's going to be? I thought they were going to come yesterday, but they never showed. I waited and waited."

"Let me give them a ring." Stella stepped into the hall to call the crime scene manager.

"Are you up to answering a few questions?" Jordan asked. "I know you've already been through it but it might jog your memory about something new. It'll help me anyway to hear it from you directly."

He went through the routine, but Julie had no idea who the intruder had been. She didn't know anyone who would have wanted to upset her, and nothing was missing as far as she had been able to tell. "I haven't looked everywhere but, like, the telly, the sound system, all that stuff is okay."

"What about a computer?" Jordan pointed to the desk in a corner that held a keyboard and mouse.

"Ha, I was lucky there. I was having some work done on it, so it wasn't here. That's just my workspace. I can't be doing with that little laptop keyboard and the track pad so I've got peripherals to plug in. I had my jewellery with me. Not that I've got much anyway, but my rings and stuff. Thank God."

"Was there any money?"

"No. Course not. We were on holiday so I took all I had with me. It's not like I have wads of cash under the mattress. I had my holiday money with me changed to euros, but there was none in the house. I'm not stupid." She gave a bitter laugh.

She told him about her job as a financial advisor in the city. Her friend Pat who'd come to work as a secretary. She mentioned her ailing mother and a father who had left when she was a teenager. "Don't know where he is, don't want to."

Stella came back into the room as Jordan put away his notebook. "The crime scene techs are on the way. Are you sure you don't want a drink or anything?" she asked.

"No. Tell you what I do want though. I want you to find the bastard, and I want you to let me meet him so I can spit in his evil face."

"Well, we'll try and do the first bit of that; not sure about the second," Jordan said. "I see you gave the patrol yesterday a vague description?"

"Yeah, a man, running away, jeans and a dark top, that's it. I didn't see anything else. Not much help, is it?"

"Definitely a man?" Stella asked.

"How do you mean? It wasn't a woman – I can tell the difference and I chased the scum."

"No, that's not what I meant. It's just that sometimes, this sort of thing, the mess, the damage, it's kids. They egg each other on, you know, like a dare."

"No, it wasn't no kids. It was a man. Bigger than me, not as big as him and white, not – well, erm, you know, black." She nodded towards Jordan. "But a bloke. Not fat, not skinny, not old. Just dead ordinary. A bog-standard bloke."

"We'll do what we can. If his fingerprints are on the database, we'll stand a chance at least."

"Yeah. Right."

Jordan handed her his card. "If you're worried about anything, call DS May or me anytime. Anything at all that we can help with."

She pursed her lips and looked around. "You'll pick all this up for me, will you? Tell me how I can ever sleep on that mattress again – well I can't, can I? How could I when I don't know what he did up there? I'm imagining all sorts. You'll catch the bastard and give him a seeing to, will you?"

They were rescued from her increasing bitterness by the technicians in paper suits with powder and brushes and things to make the chaos in her home even worse.

* * *

"Not much to go on, is there?" Stella said as she drove away.

"Next to nothing really, and with no robbery as far as she can tell, and no actual physical harm, it's not going to be a high priority for us. It's rotten for her though. It'll be a long time before she feels safe and comfortable in her home again," Jordan said.

"Well, we'll get the reports typed up but there isn't even much to put on the system. It's frustrating, makes you feel like a waste of space."

It wasn't the best start to his posting, but they called into the supermarket to pick up doughnuts for the team, most of whom he knew from his previous stint at Copy Lane.

The day was spent reviewing ongoing cases, some of which he'd be involved with. There was a call from St Anne Street with the date for a court case he'd be required to attend. It was unsatisfying, and he was glad to go home at the end of shift.

A couple of hours later he was roused from a nap on the settee by his phone rattling across the coffee table.

"Carr."

"Sergeant Flowers here, crime scene investigation. I've just sent some images to your email address. Thought I'd give you a heads-up as well. It's the robbery in Old Roan. Something odd we found in the chaos of the bedroom. The woman, Julie Scott, confirmed the stuff wasn't hers and she'd never seen it before. Freaked her out, quite understandably. I'll be available in the morning if you want a word about it, but I'm off for a bevvy now. I thought I'd let you know so you didn't feel the need to interrupt my drinking." He laughed.

"Intriguing. What is it?"

"Best you just have a look. There are four pictures. Found the things under the pillows on the bed. They're bagged and tagged so you can meet them tomorrow."

He rang off with another laugh. Jordan cleared a space on the dining table for his laptop.

Chapter 5

Given a choice, Jordan would not have shown the images to Penny, but she came into the room and peered over his shoulder. She made a noise. It was more the sound of distaste than a deliberate comment. Jordan glanced at her and then clicked through the short slideshow.

There were two small figures, made from a soft substance; cotton, or felt. One was just under thirty centimetres long and ten at the widest part of the torso. There was a ruler beside it and an evidence marker on the sheet which covered the bed. The face was flat, the large eyes were made of plastic and had pins stuck into them. A mouth had been drawn on using a pen or felt-tip pen. It was twisted into an evil grin. There were horns stitched to the top of the head. The doll had woollen hair in straight strands and wore a blue dress with a short jacket over it.

The second figure was much smaller and dressed in a white onesie. The hair was short, and the mouth downturned. Teardrops had been stitched into the face. In the tiny hand was a long pin with a bead at the end. On the larger figure, there were long pins in both eyes. It was nasty and shocking.

Jordan saved the images and forwarded them to Stella, though he assumed the scene technician would have already done that.

> *Meet you tomorrow. Off out to see Ms Scott. I'll give her a ring before I leave. I'm thinking about half eight.*

He clicked off the machine. There was nothing to be done about it tonight and although it was horrible for the victim, it was something to focus on. It could be a good thing.

* * *

Julie looked even worse than she had the day before. Her eyes were red-rimmed and sore. She hadn't changed her clothes and the coffee table was littered with cups. A bottle and glass sat in sticky rings on a side table. The house felt closed up and stale. The suitcase in the hall was pushed against the wall. The lid was open, and clothes were piled beside it on the carpet.

"Can I get you anything, Julie?" Stella asked.

The other woman shook her head quickly before leaning back on the sofa. Her hair was lank and greasy. Mascara, which must have been applied in the hotel in Spain, was smudged and clogged on her lashes.

"Have you slept?" Jordan asked.

"No, I haven't. I can't go up there. I don't know what to do. I can't bear it. What did that mean, those things?

Were they voodoo dolls; is that what they were? Is someone putting a death wish on me or something? I'm scared about what else I might find."

Stella leaned forward. "You don't need to worry about that. I've spoken to the crime scene sergeant. They looked everywhere, but there's nothing. Listen, why don't I go upstairs with you now? We can go into the bedroom together and then, if you like, I'll sit up there while you have a shower, and change your clothes. If you think it will help, we can arrange for a family liaison officer to come and stay with you today and then you could try and get some rest." She turned to Jordan. "That's okay, isn't it, boss?"

"Yes," he said, "or you can stay, Stella. I'll get back to the station and start to find out what this is, whether we've seen anything like it before and chivvy the lab along for forensics. There could be DNA on this, Julie. Try to think of it as a good thing. It's going to be more helpful to us than the nothing we had yesterday. I know it's creepy, I understand why you're upset, but honestly, it could be a help."

Julie looked up at him, sighed and stood from the settee. "I'd love a shower. I've gone through my case, and I've got some clean clothes in there. They'll do me until tomorrow, but then I'm going back to work. I need to wash my work stuff. I can't wear anything that was in the house when he came."

"Okay, well let's get on with it. You'll feel better doing something. Come on." Stella led her upstairs.

Jordan collected his laptop and phone and was on his way out of the door when Stella ran back down the stairs.

"I told her I'd put her washing on for her. This is what she always wears for work. Says it saves trying to choose something in the morning. She's got four all about the same."

She held up a hanger holding a blue dress with a short jacket over it.

Chapter 6

By the time Stella arrived back at the station, Jordan had already started his research. He had John Grice, the detective constable, and a couple of civilian clerks helping him.

They had a whiteboard with a picture of the dolls from Julie's house. "They're grotty things, aren't they? Spooky," Stella said.

"They are, but unfortunately not that unusual; the internet is full of this stuff," Jordan said. "We've concentrated on any connected with recent cases in the UK otherwise it'd be impossible. They pop up here and there, often in situations involving stalking, threats and so on. Some are at the scene of more serious crimes. I don't know how much it will help, to be honest. I reckon we need to have a longer chat with Julie when she settles a bit. She said she knew of nobody who would have broken in, but that was before we found the figures. This could have changed things. It's sinister, puts a different slant on the break-in, and makes it more threatening."

They found no local reports of dolls being left at the scenes of break-ins or robberies, though the rest of the vandalism was all too common.

Jordan would leave work early, have a word with Julie Scott on the way home, and then write his report. He needed something more to tell her than what he had found. She would eventually get over the upset, probably. She wouldn't have an improved opinion of the police, though, if they didn't solve this thing. So much for the DCI and his public relations exercise.

Steve Castle, the desk sergeant on duty, was apologetic when he rang through from reception. "I've got a woman here demanding to speak to you, sir. A Mrs Scott, says she's had a break-in. She's in a bit of a state right now. I've put her in the visitor's lounge with a constable and a cup of tea, but she wants to see you and says she's not leaving until she does.

The healthy tan that Julie had brought back from her holiday was fading already. Her skin looked dull and yellow. She had tied her hair into a ponytail but wore no make-up and had pulled a padded jacket over her casual trousers and top.

"Julie, what can I do for you?" Jordan asked.

She held out her hand. In her shaking fingers was a freezer bag and inside was a small bundle wrapped in a piece of fabric.

Jordan shook his head. "Just put it on the table, would you?"

Julie tipped the bag, and as the cloth unfolded, he could make out another doll. This one was the size of the larger one found in the bedroom, but there were no pins in the eyes. He leaned down and used a pen to move away the wrapping. This doll was dressed in a plain white smock. It had a hole where the heart would have been, and what looked like blood had been dripped across the torso.

"That was pushed through my letter box about half an hour ago. Not long after your sergeant left."

* * *

A scene of crime technician photographed the morbid little parcel, then bagged and tagged it, and took it away. Julie was given tea and refused to call anyone. Stella sat with her in the visitor's lounge.

"You didn't see anyone outside when this was left?" she asked.

"No. I was in the kitchen. I just wanted to start getting things sorted a bit. I didn't want to, but it won't do itself, will it?" She stopped and sighed. "Anyway, I heard the letter box rattle. When I saw the thing on the hall carpet, it gave me the willies straight away. I got a dustpan because first of all, I thought it was dog poo or something. Kids have done that before, the little sods. I saw what it was when I tried to brush it up."

"Did you touch it, with your fingers?"

"I didn't want to, but it was impossible. I had to wrap that hankie or whatever it is back around it. I just touched the edge and slid it into that bag."

"We've already taken your fingerprints, but I wonder if you'd let us have a DNA sample as well. Just so we know which traces are yours."

"I don't know. I mean, that makes me feel like a criminal. It will feel as though I have a record."

Stella shook her head. "No, you won't have any sort of record, not at all. Once we've sorted all this out, the DNA will be destroyed."

"Well, I suppose there's not much choice. I just don't know who the hell would want to do something like this. I mean, it's horrible."

Stella asked again about Julie's ex-husband, but he was long gone, and she was insistent that they had no contact. The split had been acrimonious. "We should never have got married and I think he was bitter and thought I'd trapped him. We rowed all the time, and I wouldn't toe the line. He turned into a proper bastard if I'm honest. He got a new job as an excuse to get away. It's a long story and old news now. But I just haven't heard from him for ages. I don't even know where he is. He could be in Timbuktu. We haven't spoken for well over ten years. I don't think he's interested enough in me to do something like this. No, that doesn't make any sense, that's all over."

Stella took the few details she could. There was an old mobile phone number and the address of Julie's ex brother-in-law, which was possibly still current.

"What are you going to do? Are you just going to stick this in a box somewhere and forget about it, about me?"

"No, we'll have a word with the DCI and see where he thinks we should take it. We've already been doing some research."

Julie was surprised by the remark. She raised her eyebrows and nodded. "Oh, well that's good. I didn't think you'd do anything."

"We'll do what we can. In the meantime, Julie, you must be careful. Make sure you lock up at night, don't leave doors open during the day. I don't want to frighten you, but until we have an idea about what's going on, just be alert."

"Shit, you don't want to scare me. Well, you have done now."

"Is there nobody you can go and stay with for a while?"

"I already said. I'm not doing that. Anyway, I'm back at work tomorrow. I'll be fine then."

Later, in the incident room, Stella and Jordan tossed ideas back and forth and apart from agreeing it was bloody odd, they couldn't make any sense of it all.

"Let's just wait and see what the forensic laboratory finds," Jordan said, "although I can't imagine what that might be. Anyway, I'm in court tomorrow and we might have something more to work with when the scene team have had a bit more time to look at things. As for the dolls, if we can get an idea where the horrible things came from, we might have a starting point at least."

"But we're taking it on, aren't we? We are going to investigate. She's at risk, surely. This mustn't be just swept under the table as another odd case."

"No, I didn't mean that at all. I'll have a word with the DCI and let him know we want to have a deeper look at it. It's still really a home invasion and then harassment, but I'll do what I can."

Chapter 7

Even as he updated reports and prepared for his court appearance in the morning, Julie and the dolls niggled at Jordan's mind.

The DCI wasn't convinced. Jordan understood that he had more to deal with than a distressed and frightened woman, and even though he showed Josh Lewis pictures of the dolls, he didn't take it as seriously. "It's somebody playing silly buggers. You think black magic and voodoo is going on in the Old Roan? I know break-ins are distressing and this is a bit over the top, but we have to keep a sense of proportion here." He paused and bent to look more closely at the images. "On the other hand, who knows, there are all sorts of nutters out there these days. I don't mind you giving her a call and maybe sending an officer round to give her some hints on security and what have you."

"She's really scared, sir."

"I don't doubt it. So are the little old ladies who have been mugged for their pensions, and the old codgers who've been thumped in the street just for looking the wrong way at a gang of thugs, or for wearing red instead of blue. It's rotten and I wish we had the capacity to look after everyone the way they would like us to. That's not the way it is, and to be honest, I reckon it's going to get worse. I'm sorry, Jordan, I know you care and it's a credit to you, but don't let yourself get too fixated on this."

Left with no other option, Jordan passed the message onto Stella and arranged for a security visit for Julie. He could imagine her reaction to that.

"I suppose that's it then," Stella said. "We give her a case number for her insurance and file it away. It's not good enough, is it?"

"I'll pop in and see her in a couple of days. I'll just make sure she's okay and reassure her that if she needs to get in touch, we're still here," Jordan said.

"It was pretty grim, though, that last doll. There's no easy way to trace the origin. They are working on the fabric and the pins, but thoughts, at the moment, are that they are pretty average. There's been a bit of an uptick in dressmaking and crafting in recent years and there are tons of places online where you can buy fabric and stuffing and all the bits and pieces you need."

"It's been homemade though, hasn't it?"

"Well, there may be places you can order voodoo dolls and black magic stuff – well of course there are, you can buy anything these days. Even then they are going to be homemade by someone, aren't they? Hardly likely to have a little label on the side, made in Croxteth, are they?"

"Croxteth, why there?" Jordan asked. "Is there a history of this sort of thing in Croxteth?"

"No, of course, there isn't, it was just the first place that sprung to mind."

"Oh right. I just wondered."

"I've been trawling the net and there are a few places offering spell removals and psychic reading and what have you," Stella said, "but I haven't seen any evidence that it's a whole underworld around here. Well, no more than anywhere else. Apart from that, surely Julie would have said if she had been exposed to something like that."

"Yes. I expect so. I have to say though that I'm unhappy about how we're leaving this."

Chapter 8

Jordan came out of the court with a grin on his face. The blokes they'd just seen sent down were evil. There was still work ongoing in Europe, but at least from their end they had been able to lock up a gang of vile abusers of women and it felt good.

"Time for a bevvy?" DCI Griffiths asked. "This could be the last case you'll be involved in for Serious and Organised. I still think you're making a mistake, but it's up to you."

"Yeah," Jordan said, "let's have a quick one. You know, don't you, that I enjoyed working for you?"

His ex-boss shrugged. "Well stay with us then."

"Nah, I'll give it some time. I think it will suit me better being at Copy Lane."

"What have you got on?"

He had to ask, didn't he?

"Well, it's early days. I've got a nasty break-in to look at and a local gang of car thieves causing trouble. Problems with groups of girls shoplifting in the chemists."

"Shit, Jordan, you can do better than that. You're wasting your talents. Break-ins and car thieves, shoplifting, for God's sake."

He was saved from further argument by the burble of his phone. "It's Stella, I'll catch you up."

Griffiths stomped away.

In the event, they never had the drink.

He took the call and sent a text to Griffiths. His car was parked at St Anne Street, and he struggled against the urge to run on the way back there. It wouldn't make any difference and he would look like a prat pounding the streets in his suit.

In his locker at Copy Lane were spare clothes, and once he had changed, he texted Penny to say he would probably be late.

He knew what to expect, but turning into the road in Old Roan was still surreal given how recently they had been there. Stella waved to him from near the tea van. As he crossed the road, she spoke to the guy behind the counter. The drink would be stewed and bitter, but it would be warm and give him something to do with his hands while she brought him up to date.

They flashed their warrant cards at the officer with the clipboard and he stood aside to allow them access. "Safe route there, CSI are inside. The coroner is on his way," he said. "The next-door neighbour found her and called it in. She heard a disturbance and came to investigate. An officer is with her, she's very shaken. We've sent for her son. The patrol who were first on the scene are round the back."

The house was a little tidier than it had been. Some of the broken ornaments had been cleared away and the cups moved from the side tables. There were a couple of boxes in the hall with the name of a charity shop on them. Jordan and Stella didn't go into the kitchen. There was no need and no point. Julie lay on the rug. There was a great deal of blood.

Next door, Mrs Jones was distraught. "Poor Julie, she's dead isn't she. I know she is. I didn't touch her. I couldn't bear to. All that blood."

"I'm afraid she is deceased, yes," Jordan said.

He interviewed her gently, but all she could tell him was that she heard a noise and, after the events of a couple of days before, had knocked on Julie's door.

"I went round the back. I saw her through the kitchen door, it was unlocked, and I went in," she said and then she began to cry.

"You didn't see anyone else?"

"No, nobody."

"You didn't hear a car?"

"No. Just this noise, shouting. I was a bit scared after that bloke the other day, so I didn't go straight away. I just stood in the hallway and waited and listened. I should have gone round sooner, shouldn't I?"

"I don't think it would have made any difference and you did all that you could do. The main thing is that you're okay. I'm going to have this officer stay with you until your son arrives and then tomorrow, or whenever you feel ready, we'll have someone take a statement," Jordan said.

"I've told you it all already," she said.

"I know, I know, but we have to have it put down officially. Don't worry about it now."

Chapter 9

Back in the station, they immediately set to work. They set up a whiteboard and asked for technicians to arrange more workspaces. Jordan brought DCI Josh Lewis up to speed. He needed a team and wanted to know how many personnel he could hope for. He knew it would be a difficult conversation, and it was every bit as bad as he expected.

He didn't know the DCI well, but he had never thought of him as having sloping shoulders. Today, though, there was the feeling that he was going for an arm's-length approach. He didn't go as far as denying knowledge of the problem, but it was hinted that Jordan had failed to alert him to the seriousness of the situation.

It was annoying and frustrating. It was unfair. But Jordan was still reeling from the sight of Julie Scott's body in a pool of blood.

Jordan would have more respect for his superior officer if he'd been upfront about the fact that he needed somewhere to shift the blame. It was obvious he was reacting to messages that were coming down from higher up the food chain. A murder was bad enough, but the murder of someone they were already supposed to be helping made for very bad press, and it wouldn't be long before the headlines started to appear.

Jordan could have pointed out that he'd been told to back off. He could remind his boss that he'd tried to elevate the investigation into something more important. Anything he said would sound feeble, however. He didn't want to do that. He would sound weak, so he kept his mouth shut. He settled for agreeing where he had to and letting the rest of it hit him squarely on the chin. Apart from anything else, he felt that blame and finger-pointing didn't matter. Julie Scott was dead. She had been a nice woman who had come to them for help, and they had failed her. He had failed her.

When he left the DCI's office, he took a moment to calm himself. He would tell Stella that they could have a team including John Grice, Kath Webster and Violet Purcell, junior officers they'd both worked with before, and any clerical staff that could be taken from other cases. He wouldn't tell her about the rest of the conversation. She was already deeply upset. She had brushed away tears as they stood outside the house at the Old Roan.

"Jesus, we have screwed up now. That poor bloody woman. Talk about dropping the ball. What are we for, Jordan? Really, what are we for if we can let this happen?"

He didn't know what to say to her. She was right.

Now it was all about justice. The only thing they could do was to find the perpetrator.

Chapter 10

Stella turned from where she stood in front of her desk, still reeling. "God, Jordan, how has this happened? What did we miss?"

"We need to just take a minute, mate. Then we have to go back to the beginning. There was the break-in, we did what we could. I know that was very little given the sparsity of information and the total lack of any clues. We did react to the dolls. Well, we started to, but this has all happened so quickly and it's a bloody shock. A horrible bloody shock. Get onto the lab, tell them to put a push on the examination of the dolls. We'll assemble the team as quickly as possible and have a briefing this afternoon to get everyone up to speed. I'm going through my notes now and I think you should do the same. Look at the interviews with Julie. If we missed anything, we must be upfront about it. Guilt and regret are going to get us nowhere now."

"You're right, I'll tell you who isn't human, though, the bloody pervert who sent her those dolls, the evil scroat who has done this."

"Let's not make any assumptions either. It would make sense that there is a connection between the break-in, the dolls, and the murder, but don't close off any avenues in your mind."

"Oh, come on. Of course they're connected. What are you saying? Julie Scott was an ordinary woman, she was getting, what appear to be, black magic threats or something to do with all that off-the-wall stuff, and someone else just came in and killed her?"

"I don't know, Stella. That's the point. We don't know and we will find out."

She shook her head as she turned and walked away from him.

The room was filling with the team. Computer engineers were crawling under the desks, chairs were being dragged in from empty offices and the atmosphere was one of anger and shock, but also a subdued excitement. Thankfully, cases of murder were still relatively rare. There had been the chance that some of the people now milling around might never have worked on one through their whole careers. But that wasn't to be. Jordan had worked with some of them before and thought he could rely on them. He made some notes ready for the briefing and then nipped out and came back with a pile of pizza boxes, a crate of water, and one of cola.

"Okay, grab a slice and a drink and we'll get on with this. The first hours are the most important – we all know that. However, in this case, we are possibly already lagging behind. This could certainly have started a few days ago. There was no way to know how it would turn out, and now we are playing catch-up. As soon as I hear they have moved the body, I'm going over to the house to have another look around. In the meantime, DS May will give you tasks. DC Grice, John, next of kin haven't been informed. Her mother is still alive but ill. I believe she is in hospital right now."

"She's been released, boss," Grice said.

"Okay, that's good but I still don't think there's any need to have her identify the body, we have prints, we do have her DNA but that'll take a while to check. Anyway, we met her a few days ago. That should ease things for the family, but I still have to go and speak to the mother. We should visit the friend she was on holiday with. I want to get to that before they see it on the news, and we've asked the press office to make sure her name isn't released until we give them the all-clear. Of course neighbours are going to put two and two together, so we need to move quickly. Get me addresses. Actually, John, will you speak to the friend? We need to find out if anything that could have a bearing on this happened on the holiday. Find out whether she said anything to indicate that she was worried, frightened or having trouble with anyone. She told us no, but she might have been more open with her mate. Then we need door-to-door as soon as possible. I'll see if I can rope in some uniforms to help with that. But a high priority is the mother. Get on that first. Dr Jasper has agreed to rush the post-mortem examination through for us. I feel that we are firefighting a bit here. When the press finds out that she had already been in touch and more than once, they'll likely have a field day. I want to make decent progress as quickly as we can."

"Okay, boss. I'll have that for you soon as."

"Good man. Now, this is what we know."

Chapter 11

Post-mortems were probably the least favourite part of the job for Jordan. They were unavoidable however, and though he wasn't squeamish about the smells and the sights, it was the assault on the body of the victim that upset him. The medical examiners were respectful, even the taciturn and cranky James Jasper. It helped, but it was still a trial for Jordan to see the chest opened, remains dissected, the body parts weighed and pored over.

He could have sent someone else and simply read the report, but he needed to be there in case there were questions; anyway, it was his job. Stella came with him. She stood for a moment in silence with her head bowed and the others in the room saw and paused until she looked up and blushed slightly to see that they had noticed.

Dr Jasper was known for his abrupt attitude and impatience. People attending one of his examinations for the first time wondered how the staff in the morgue put up with his temper and sarcasm. Those who had been around a while knew that he was outstanding in the field and his lectures were always oversubscribed. Professionalism and respect won the day.

Jordan held to the idea that the gruff demeanour was mostly a ploy to control the atmosphere in the room. He had spent an evening with Jasper at an event hosted by Citizens Advice Bureau and the doctor, though not jovial exactly, was pleasant company and empathetic when talking to Jordan's wife about the problems the Citizens Advice people had to deal with in their jobs. Throwing instruments at the wall and shouting at the assistants gave people who might find the procedure hard to handle something other to think about than the victim on the table. Jack Carter, his usual assistant had worked with him for years and let the bluster flow straight over his head, occasionally raising an eyebrow if he thought the boss had gone too far.

As usual, there were a couple of students with him. They were past the stage when they might pass out or run for the toilets once the cutting started, but they stood back reverently until he called them forward to 'Get a proper look' at something.

This time was harder than usual for the police. They had known this woman. Only briefly and only as part of the job, but they were tormented by the idea that she was in the morgue because they had failed her. Jordan knew this thinking wasn't going to help, but convincing himself and everyone else that he had done all he could was impossible right then.

He pushed the niggling thoughts aside to concentrate on the commentary by Jasper. Death was due to a wound in the chest. The medical examiner posited that the blow had punctured the aorta most likely by chance.

"Bloody unlucky, a bit to either side and the sod would have missed. She died quickly but not instantly. There is something else though. I have found threads in and around the wound."

"Threads?" Jordan said.

"Yes, I would think, from experience that it is towelling or something like that. To me, that suggests that maybe someone tried to help this woman. Maybe they tried to staunch the bleeding and when they were unsuccessful, they gave up and ran. You should probably look for blood-soaked cloths, but I suppose I don't need to tell you something so obvious."

They already knew that a knife was missing from the kitchen block, and it was confirmed the wound could have been made by a blade the length and width of the one that would fit the space.

"These bloody blocks are available everywhere. I don't know why anyone would have them sitting out like that," growled the doctor. "They are there on the worktop and one or two knives are used regularly. The rest of them are simply waiting to be abused. This is the one they call the 'chef's knife' – God knows why – who's the bloody chef and what chef has one knife? It's to give the punters ideas about themselves. Anyway, wherever it is, when you find that you'll have your murder weapon. It's not a complicated death this, Jordan." He glanced up and peered over his glasses. "Simply – bloody murder. Stabbed with a knife and bled to death. I'll send a report, but it's not going to tell you anything that you couldn't see right at the crime scene. *Why* is another matter, and that's your job. I don't envy you."

There was no point in them staying longer. Jordan and Stella left the bright tiled room to the experts who would make Julie suitable for viewing.

Chapter 12

It took Julie's mother a while to answer when Jordan rang the bell at the neat semi in Aintree. It wasn't far from her daughter's house.

He was about to ring again when he saw a small silhouette through the window beside the front door. Doris Beetham opened the door a crack, the security chain stretched tautly. The old woman was pale and drawn. Her grey hair was cut in a short bob, and as she peered at them, she tucked it behind her ears. She wore a soft pink tracksuit with a long black cardigan draped across her shoulders. She pulled it tighter to her as she leaned forward, the better to see them. It was hard to judge her age; her face was wrinkled but her eyes were bright and clear, and she held herself straight. She was slim and petite. According to DC John Grice, she was in her eighties.

Jordan already had his warrant card held in front of him. As she undid the security chain and pulled open the door, she sighed, her eyes filled with tears. It was a puzzle to him how people often knew before a word had been spoken. They had a sixth sense that those on their doorstep were bringing the worst of news.

Doris Beetham straightened up to her full height of a metre and a half and squared her shoulders. She looked frail. According to DC Grice, her stay in hospital had been for minor heart surgery, and they debated whether it was safe to visit her without medical backup.

Jordan's main concern was that he had the chance to speak to her before her daughter's name was released to the media. Now she simply nodded at them once, turned and walked down her narrow hallway and into the living room. She left them to enter the house and close the door behind them.

By the time they joined her, she was sitting on the settee in the tidy living room with a glass of water in one hand and a tissue clutched in the fingers of the other.

She turned and looked at them. "Tell me quickly. Don't mess about."

"Mrs Beetham, is there anyone who can be with you?" Stella said.

"Just tell me. Was it an accident? She was in Spain, my daughter. It is my Julie you've come about, isn't it?"

"I'm afraid it is," Jordan said.

"It wasn't a plane crash; I'd have heard about that. Even in the hossie, I'd have heard about that. So, what then? A car accident. I've told her and told her. You be careful, Julie, them foreign drivers are mad, and they drive on the wrong side of the road. 'Oh, Mum,' she'd say. 'Oh, Mum, don't be so daft, it's not the wrong side of the road for them.' Ha, well. She's dead, isn't she? My girl is dead."

Jordan sat beside her on the settee. Stella went into the kitchen and filled the kettle.

"When did you last hear from Julie, Mrs Beetham?" Jordan asked quietly.

"Not since she went away." The dam broke and tears flooded down her cheeks as she leaned forward over her knees and began to sob.

"Can I call your doctor, Mrs Beetham," Jordan said. "Is there anyone who can come and look after you?"

"No, not just now. I don't need the doctor." She reached out to a side table and picked up a packet of pills. She popped one from the blister pack and swallowed it with a gulp of water. Her face was wet with tears and her breathing was shallow and fast with, every now and then, a deep sob.

Jordan sat beside her. He wanted to reach out and take her hand, to put his arm around her thin shoulders and offer the comfort he would have given to his mother, to his nana, but it wasn't possible, so he sat in silence. He was close, so if she reached for him, he was there.

She gathered herself and turned to him. "Tell me then, lad. Tell me what happened. I have to know. First of all, where is she? Is she still in Spain?"

As bad as this had been, Jordan knew that he was about to make it worse. He moved his hand nearer, and she took it and clutched it with her tiny old lady fingers.

"She's in the UK. Your daughter didn't die in Spain, Mrs Beetham. She died in her own home."

"Oh no. I could have spoken to her. If I'd got myself sorted and not been such a wuss, I could have spoken to her. But…" She paused. "In her own home? Round the corner there? In her house?"

Jordan nodded and gave it another moment and watched as the horror dawned. "Not, that murder. She's not that murder? That was on the news? Oh, no, don't tell me that. I heard it in the hospital. We all said how horrible it was that it was here close by. But no, tell me it's not that."

Chapter 13

There was much that Jordan needed to ask Julie's mother but by the time Stella came back from the kitchen with a mug of tea, Doris's hands were shaking uncontrollably. The tea splashed out onto her trousers. She had become quiet now, the earlier chattering gave way to silent weeping.

"I'm going to ring your doctor if you don't mind. Just to let him know you've had a nasty shock. Ask him to pop in and make sure you're okay," Jordan said.

"Ha, chance'd be a fine thing. Days when they come to the house are long gone, lad. Not here anyway. No, I'm all right. Could you knock next door? Ginny Barnes'll come and sit with me."

Stella left the room. They heard the front door open and a few minutes later she was back with a neighbour in tow.

The woman was younger than Doris Beetham but still past retirement age. Jordan stood aside so that she could sit on the settee, and as she wrapped her arms around the older woman's shoulders Doris gave way to the anguish, repeating her daughter's name over and over.

"We'll need to come back," Jordan said. "Maybe tomorrow. We will have some questions. We want to find out what happened to Julie as quickly as possible, and Doris may have some information that'll help."

"All right," Ginny said. "Take my number and let me know when you're coming. I'll make sure she's not on her own. I'm going to stay with her now and see if she'll come to mine tonight. She's not a well woman. What the hell happened here? Last I heard Julie was off in Spain with that friend of hers. That whatsername."

"Pat Roach," Stella said.

"Aye, her – slag!"

Jordan raised his eyebrows but resisted commenting. John Grice should have interviewed the woman by now. It was going to be interesting to get his impressions.

They left the two women and headed back to the station. Most of the civilian staff had gone, but John Grice and the two juniors, Kath and Vi, were still working.

"Let's go over what we've got today and then, does anyone fancy a bevvy?" Jordan said.

"Great. How was the post-mortem?" Kath asked. "I know it was probably horrible but what did we learn?"

"Not much new really," Jordan answered. "We now have confirmation of the murder weapon but unless we find it, that's not much help."

32

"The DCI was in earlier," John Grice said. "He left you a message, there's a note on your desk. He said he'll try and free up some uniforms for the house-to-house and the evidence search."

"Excellent news. How did you get on with your interview with her friend?"

"She wasn't there. She was supposed to be in work but hadn't turned up. I went round to the house and rang her mobile. I couldn't find her."

"Right. Well, that's interesting. Did you glean anything from her colleagues?"

"I did have a short chat with a couple of them. Of course, they were all in a bit of a state about Julie. One or two reckoned that's why Pat wasn't at work. Too cut up about her friend. Then again, the boss was of a different opinion."

"How so?" Jordan said.

"He said he never saw what they had in common and couldn't understand the friendship. He had a lot of regard for Julie, for Pat not so much. She hadn't been there as long and was in a much less responsible job. She wasn't particularly reliable and had been on report a couple of times for bits and pieces like poor timekeeping and absenteeism. His words were that they were like chalk and cheese. Julie was better paid and had better prospects. He thought she might find Pat's way of life more exciting than hers. Julie was quiet, a homebody by all accounts, and Pat liked clubbing and drinking."

"That's interesting. We need to find Pat Roach," Jordan said. "You and Vi will make it your priority tomorrow. If you don't have any luck in the usual places, we might have to step it up a bit. If they were close enough friends to go away together, it's odd for her to vanish just now."

"Unless she's scared," Stella said.

"Yes, or guilty of something," Kath added.

Chapter 14

It was late when Jordan arrived back in Crosby and Penny had gone to bed. A pork casserole was in the oven waiting to be reheated, but he'd given in to temptation after the drinks in the pub and gone to the chip shop with the others. He covered the dish and put it in the fridge.

As he slid into bed beside his wife, warm and fresh from the shower, she murmured and turned towards him. "S'late."

"Yes. Sorry I went for a drink."

"Worried," she muttered.

He pulled her close. Penny was strong and never verbalised the worry that he knew she carried with her constantly. He appreciated it but was hurt that he was the cause of it.

"Everything's fine, love. All good," he said.

She was already deeply asleep and snoring gently. He mentally kicked himself for not sending her a text. He was often late. It was par for the course, but it would have been kinder to let her know he wasn't anywhere in trouble. So, while he was sitting in the pub with his pint of IPA, Penny had been at home worrying. He screwed his eyes up at the wave of guilt. He'd apologise to her in the morning when she was properly awake. He'd do better.

His phone rang just after five in the morning. Stella apologised for disturbing him but said that she was sure he'd want to know what was going on. "I'll be with you in twenty minutes," he told her.

The apology would have to wait. He gathered his clothes and carried them into the bathroom. Dressed and back in the bedroom, he kissed his sleeping wife and, carefully so he didn't wake him, he stroked Harry's face. He left a note on the breakfast bar.

Stella was already outside the house in Old Roan when he arrived. She held out a takeaway coffee.

"What's going on?" Jordan said.

"The bobby on the door heard a noise. He's switched on, thank goodness. Went to have a look and disturbed someone in the back, trying to gain access. They've broken the pane of glass beside the door. I guess they would have got in if they'd had more time. Anyway, they ran off. We've put out an alert, but he didn't get much of a look. Male, he thinks, dark clothes, average height, average weight. It was funny but he said he was just 'bog-standard'."

Stella paused to see if her words had the effect she expected.

"Bog-standard. That's just what Julie said about the man she chased when she came back from her holiday, isn't it?"

Stella nodded. "I wondered if you'd catch on. Thought you would. Is it the same person? If it is, he's willing to take quite a risk to gain access. With a bobby on the front door and all."

"We need to get the technicians out here to see if they can find any prints."

"I've left a message. Told them it's urgent."

"Of course you have." Jordan smiled at her. "I guess we might as well have a quick look inside, seeing as we're here now. Although he didn't get in?"

"No. What the hell is there in this place that he wants so badly?"

The house was just as they had last seen it. They took pictures of the damaged window, even though the technicians would do that anyway. "It's going on seven. Do you fancy breakfast somewhere?"

"Great. I know a café on Altway; they do an ace sausage and egg bap."

Chapter 15

Back in the incident room, they noted the latest development on the board. The DCI had been as good as his word and the space was crowded with uniformed officers.

"Thanks for coming in, guys. I know some of you are giving up your days off and I appreciate it," Jordan said. "There will be overtime pay, but I don't know for how long so let's make sure we make the best of the time we have. DS May and DC Grice are in charge of assigning tasks. Mostly it will be pretty routine. House-to-house with the usual questions. We need to know about the day of the murder, but don't forget there was a break-in while Julie Scott was on holiday. It could have been a coincidence that he was there when she walked in, just bad timing. He ran, so it doesn't seem that he meant her harm, but let's not rule anything out. Did the neighbours know the times she was away? They might have spoken about it to their friends. Did anyone see suspicious activity? Was there a man hanging around? That goes for yesterday. Julie's house backs onto a small access road for the shops. There are houses there as well. Did anyone see a bloke running away this morning?"

"Have we got a description?" someone asked.

"Yes, average height, average weight, average clothes. Shouldn't be too difficult to track down." Jordan was rewarded with a ripple of quiet laughter. "Seriously, it was male, and we think IC1, reasonably fit from the way he had it on his toes. The officer at the house said it was about four this morning. On the one hand, it means that not many people would be about but anyone who was, especially someone running and not togged out in Lycra, would be noticed. We could be lucky.

"As for the search, you've all got a mock-up image of the sort of knife we're looking for. We are also searching for towels or that sort of thing covered in blood. I'm sorry but it's bins and bags as well as yards and bushes, so, let's get on with it. Good luck."

As the troops filed out, Jordan turned to Stella. "Have we had nothing more back about the dolls, yet?"

"Only the preliminary reports. I'll chase the lab today."

"John, ring Pat Roach's office today. If she's not there, go to her home. If she's still missing. I'm going to get an alert out for her. If we work quickly, we could get an appeal on the rolling news by this afternoon. Just a request for her to get in touch at the moment. If that doesn't work, we'll have to go for an all-ports alert."

"What's your thinking there, boss?" Grice asked.

"Not sure. Could be she is really upset, as some of her colleagues thought. Could simply be that she's gone off somewhere and doesn't realise we need to talk to her. Or…"

"Shit, boss, do you think she could have been involved in killing her mate?"

"The medical examiner wouldn't rule out the idea that the killer could have been a strong woman. Of course, there is the other possibility. Heaven forbid but could we have another victim?"

"I bloody hope not," Stella said.

"Yes, I guess we all hope not. I have to admit, whatever the reason for her disappearance, I'll be relieved to see her alive and well," Jordan said.

Chapter 16

Jordan would have preferred to be out in the streets helping with the door-to-door inquiries but he stayed at his desk. That wasn't his job anymore, and anyway, Josh Lewis wanted a report.

The boss didn't offer coffee, although he sat with him in the informal part of the office. Mixed messages put Jordan on alert. "I managed to arrange for some help," Lewis said.

"Yes, thank you, sir. We have everyone out already, the whole team. Stella is helping with the house-to-house."

"Excellent. The problem we have here…" Lewis paused. "This looks very bad for us, Jordan. I'm sure you see that. The intention was to send out a message that we were taking home break-ins seriously and what has happened is pretty much the exact opposite. We didn't solve this crime early on, and now we have a dead body. The thinking has to be that they are linked, yes?"

Jordan nodded. They'd had this conversation before and, as then, he knew pointing out he had been told to back off wasn't the way to go. "We are working as hard as we can on this, sir. Everyone is cut up about what's happened."

"I'm sure you are but what progress have you made? Is there anything I can take with me when I go to meet the chief constable later today?"

Jordan clutched at the only straw available. "Julie's friend has gone missing. I am arranging a press alert today."

"Is she a person of interest?"

"Not yet. But she hasn't turned up for work and she's not at her home. It's odd. I was hoping to tread carefully for now. There may be an innocent explanation but I'm monitoring events closely."

"Okay. Move it up a notch. Put out an all-ports alert for her. Have you got a BOLO out on her car?"

"No, as I say, I was taking things more cautiously."

"Keep me informed. I'll put a spin on this to hopefully get the chief constable off our backs for a while. We need some action, Jordan. The press hasn't let rip yet, but it won't be long before they start with banner headlines about police incompetence. I don't want that happening."

Outside his office, Karen, the secretary, was waiting. "Jordan, DS May called while you were in the meeting. Can you get back to her as soon as possible? It's to do with the house-to-house. I hope that wasn't too foul." She jerked her head towards the office door.

"No more than I expected and to be honest, he's right. He's a bit grumpy, isn't he?"

"Wife's not well. Nothing serious, hopefully, but she's having tests."

"Right. Fingers crossed for that, then."

"Oh yes. They've not been married long. His first wife died."

"Poor bugger," Jordan said.

"Well see if you can't do something to cheer him up a bit then, eh?"

Jordan knew what she meant. As he walked down the corridor, he pulled out his mobile phone and switched off the silent setting. There were three missed calls from Stella and a text.

Call me as soon as.

Chapter 17

A new development of small town houses backed onto the block of shops. The road behind this strip of nail bars, dog groomers and Chinese takeaways was accessible from the back garden of Julie's house. Their witness lived in one of the town houses. Jordan pulled in behind Stella's electric VW and by the time he had walked along the short concrete path, the door was opened.

Stella was typing on the keyboard of her tablet. She glanced up at Jordan. "Hiya, sorry about all the calls. Didn't realise you were in with the boss. How did it go?"

"Not too bad under the circumstances. I'll fill you in later. What have we got here?"

"Okay, so this lady is Gillian Lamb. She's a new mum, twins – Christ, Jordan, I don't know how people do this. Talk about exhausted."

"Yes, I remember."

"Oh, course you do. Your Harry."

"Yes, but in fairness he was a good little lad. It was just that Penny wasn't well for a while which made things tricky. But that's not important now."

"No, sorry. Anyway, Gil was up with one of her babies. She's got two boys – Jack and James. She was standing by the window rocking one of them in the early hours. Her hubby's away so it all falls to her, poor thing. But good for us, because she reckons she saw someone come over the fence at the back of the houses. She has shown me which one and it seems clear it was the one where Julie lived. It was dark and she wasn't expecting it, but she's more than fifty per cent sure it was that one. He ran down in front of the lock-ups. She couldn't see him then because of the angle but, not long after she saw a car speed out and onto the main road. No chance at all that she would get the registration and all she knows is that it was dark-coloured, hatchback type, no idea about the make."

"Are there cameras?" Jordan asked.

"Yes, I was sending a message to the council to ask for access to theirs and then we can go to the shops and see who has what. Do you want to talk to Gil first though?"

"Yes, and then we'll go and have a look at the lock-ups."

The house smelled of babies. Jordan recognised it at once.

Gil Lamb looked to be in her early twenties. She wore striped lounging trousers and a stained T-shirt. Her blond-streaked hair was pulled back in a ponytail with strands escaping and trailing around her face. She was pale, and had dark rings under her eyes.

In the corner of the room, a double stroller was draped with two blue blankets. A clothes airer visible through the kitchen doorway was filled with little onesie suits and cardigans.

"You've got your hands full," Jordan said, nodding at the baby sleeping in a crib and the other in his mother's arms.

"Yeah. It's a lot," she said. "They're brilliant, but I'd no idea how much work it would be. I wouldn't be without them, but I could do with a break now and then."

"Your husband is away."

"Yes, he had time off when they were born but he wants to save some of his paternity leave for when I get back to work. My mum helps when she can, but the nights are hard."

There was a snuffling noise from the cot in the corner and Gil glanced across the room. "Oh sugar, I just got him off and this little man needs changing."

Jordan walked to the corner. He bent down and stretched out a hand. "He's awake. Is this Jack?"

Gil laughed. "No that's James."

"Shall I pick him up? I've got a little boy of my own."

"Oh, would you. Then I can go and change Jack, and I could make us a cup of tea."

"I can do that," Stella said.

"Brilliant. Hey, you guys can come again."

"Well, I'm better at tea than babies to be honest, but he'll be okay with the boss," Stella said.

James was fascinated by this big black man lifting him. He reached out a hand and pulled at Jordan's chin.

Gil flopped down on the settee next to Jordan. "Jack's gone down for a nap. I can take him if you like." She reached for the baby.

"You have your tea, he's okay just now."

"Brilliant." She picked up the mug and settled on the settee with a sigh.

Stella was typing on the tablet. From outside there was the subdued sound of cars on the main road and the shouts of children playing somewhere. Birds tweeted on the rooves. The baby on Jordan's knee grew heavy as his eyelids lowered and his breathing deepened. Jordan turned to ask if he should put James back in his crib. Gil's eyes were closed, her mouth was slackened, and she snored quietly. The mug of tea was perched precariously on the arm of the settee. It was the first time in his career that Jordan had experienced a witness falling asleep before he had a chance to ask any questions. Stella glanced up and raised her eyebrows.

"Oh, that's not helpful," she said.

"Give her a few minutes. She's worn out and it's still early. We need to speak to her, but you've already requisitioned the CCTV downloads and until we get those there's not much more we can do. Drink your tea. We can all just take a moment."

Chapter 18

Gil Lamb coughed and jerked awake. "Oh, my God. What am I like? I am so, so sorry."

Jordan smiled at her. "You're all right. You just nodded off for a couple of minutes. You need to watch your cup."

"Oh right." She leaned and placed the now cold mug of tea on the coffee table. Her face was red, and her eyes filled with tears. "I'm so embarrassed, I don't know what's happening to me."

"Hey, don't worry. Go easy on yourself, there's no harm done. We've just been sitting here. The DS got on with a bit of work."

"But what must you think of me? You've got to think I'm a real divvy."

"No. I think you're worn out. Right now, though, your babies are asleep. Listen, you have a lie-down, we'll go and look at the lock-ups and then come back in half an hour or so."

"Wow, you are kind. Thank you. Coppers. You know people round here, a lot of 'em, they don't like coppers. I have to say I've never had any problems, but then I've never done anything wrong. But you, you're something else again."

"We're only doing what we're paid for. Looking after the public." Jordan grinned as he said it.

"Aye, well, I bet they didn't include babysitting in that when you signed up."

Stella and Jordan stood up quietly.

"You sit there, love, we'll let ourselves out and then we'll come back in a bit," Stella said. "Give me your number, I'll text you, so we don't have to ring the doorbell. You know, just in case they're still asleep."

"Ha, chance'd be a fine thing, but fingers crossed. Thank you so much."

* * *

The road behind the shops was covered in litter. The surface was pitted, and weeds sprouted along the edges. The lock-up units were the size of a one-car garage, all with timber double doors. Some had been well maintained and had hasp and staple fastenings with hefty padlocks. Some of them were not so well looked after and the doors on a couple were rotted and hanging unevenly on rusty hinges.

"We need to find out who owns these," Jordan said. "Maybe they're rented as part of shop leases. Get on to Kath and ask her to chase up copies of leases for the businesses and these units. We need names for landlords and what have you. It could be that the car was just hanging about waiting for the bloke who tried to get into Julie's, or it could be that it's stored here."

"There's a pile of fag ends here as if somebody was waiting," Stella said.

"Yes, but there's another one here. I guess the staff from the shops might leave them when they take a smoking break. Don't think it's going to help. Mind you, this might." Jordan crouched in front of one of the units. "It rained yesterday afternoon, didn't it? First time for a while?"

"Yeah, what have you found?"

"Tyre tracks here at the edge where the tarmac is crumbled. They look new, there are no others around. It might help to find out what car was here. Maybe we'll be able to match the tread pattern and wear. I'll get on to the forensic science lab. They could make a cast. I need something to cover this with, in case there's more rain or more traffic."

He was taking pictures with his phone. Stella walked to where the bins were grouped at the end of the block of garages. She rooted around for a while and came back with a broken plastic crate and a sheet of polythene. "I reckon that'll cover it for now."

"Perfect. Okay. This feels like progress of a sort. We'll have a chat with Gil. Then we'll have a word with the shopkeepers. There are flats above. They should have been covered in the house-to-house but maybe not the specific questions we need to ask about cars in the early hours. We'll get the troops back here if necessary and then Kath and Vi can start reviewing CCTV footage. On top of that, I need to move things along in the search for Pat Roach."

"Yes. We've got a bit to be going on with. Shame this didn't happen before you spoke to the DCI."

"Doesn't matter, it's happened now, and it feels as though the case is coming back to life. There's something else."

"What's that?" Stella said.

"We'd better double-check the search party had a look at these bins. Have you got any scene tape in your car?"

"Yeah, always."

"Tape off the bin store, would you? We are still looking for that knife," Jordan said, "and if this place has anything to do with what's been happening, we need to have a look. Find out when the bins were last emptied. Come on, let's get back. I could do with a cuppa, and I bet Gil won't say no. What time is it?"

"Going on half four."

"I'm going to nip round to that baker's shop on the front. I'll grab us all some iced buns or something. See you back at Gil's in ten minutes."

Chapter 19

They sat with Gil Lamb and had tea and iced buns. Jack had woken but was happy in a bouncy chair where he sat jiggling a plastic set of spoons. She didn't have much to add to what they already knew. She had seen the bloke climb over the back fence.

"He was fit, not in a fanciable way." She laughed and glanced at Stella. "I mean he was agile. He did sort of stumble when he landed, maybe he hurt himself, it made him run funny. But he didn't fall right over. Then he went straight down in front of the garages. I thought it was odd, so I watched and then a couple of minutes later I heard the car and it drove out. Fast. I thought they might have been robbing the garden sheds. That happens a lot. They pinch things like nice tools and stuff and sell them or, I suppose, they get knives and blades. It's mostly young lads and this bloke looked older. Not old but not a kid, if you know what I mean. I've thought about it a lot, and he didn't have anything in his hands. I'm sure of that. He could have had something in his pockets, I suppose. I'm not that much help, am I? Has something happened over there? On the other road. I wouldn't know, I don't go round there much but I saw police around and then you" – she nodded at Stella – "knocked on the door and so, has it? Has there been a robbery? Do I need to worry? Only, being on my own with my Kev away such a lot..."

"No, you don't need to worry. Just take the usual precautions," Jordan said. "You know the sort of thing. Lock up at night, and if you've got a burglar alarm make sure you set it. Or if you haven't got one, see about having one fitted. But there's nothing to worry about."

"Okay. So why are you going around asking questions then?"

"There has been an incident. I can't say too much about it but a woman on the other road has been found dead."

Gil covered her mouth with her hands. "Oh no. How do you mean, found dead?"

"We can't say much about it." Jordan pulled out his phone with a picture of Julie. "Do you know her? She lives in the houses over the fence."

"Oh yeah. That's Julie. I see her at the shops sometimes. Only to say hello to. Shit, she's not the one, is she? She wasn't very old at all. She was lovely."

"I'm afraid so."

"Aww. That's horrible. Poor Julie."

"How much do you know about her?" Stella asked.

"Not much. As I say, I see her at the shops now and then and she always asks how the babies are. I think she's divorced and lives on her own. That's about it really."

"And this person?" Jordan showed her the picture of Pat Roach that John Grice had managed to persuade the human resources people at the office in Liverpool to give him.

"No." Gil shook her head. "Don't know her."

"Okay then. We'll leave you in peace. I'll leave my card and if you think of anything just give us a ring. If you're worried anytime, just call either the landline or my mobile."

"I will, thanks." Gil picked up the card and slipped it into her pocket.

"Will I be able to find out when the funeral is? I'll send some flowers or something. I probably won't be able to go. Not with the babbies."

"I'll try and let you know," Jordan said.

With a final glance at the little boy, who was beginning to grizzle, they left.

"Come on," Jordan said, "let's go round and see what we can find out at the shops and then back to the station. I need to move things along."

Chapter 20

All the shops had security cameras, but the results of their requests for copies of footage were mixed. For some of them, the cameras mounted on the wall were all they had by way of a deterrent. There was no download, just a small red light to lead would-be troublemakers astray. A couple of them wiped the drives every twenty-four hours and others were staffed by people who needed permission from 'the boss' to share the recordings. Jordan wanted them on side and stopped short of threatening warrants.

The electronics shop, which was the last in the short row, gave them the best outcome. They had an up-to-date camera with a recording facility which downloaded to a computer, and there were units at both the front and back of the premises.

"We have to store some stuff in the garage," the owner told them. "It's not ideal but I've done the best I can. My insurance is through the roof, but my security is state of the art. I sell systems, if you're interested."

"Thank goodness for enthusiasts," Jordan said to Stella, as they waited for a copy of the images from the night before.

"There you go," the man said. "I haven't actually looked at it though. Well, there was no need. Nothing has happened. Although now that you've come maybe I should."

"We'll have our digital forensic department have a look. If there's anything we need to ask you about, we'll give you a bell. You've been very helpful. Thanks, Mr…"

"Brady, call me Joe."

Back at the station, the team was still working hard.

"The press section has put an appeal together for sightings of Pat Roach, boss," John Grice said. "We were hoping to get it out before the six o'clock news, so I took the liberty of giving them the go-ahead and I've said yes for a copy to go to the *Echo*. It should be on their website within the next hour and in the paper tonight. Hope that's okay. I know I should have run it past you, but you didn't answer the phone."

"It's fine, John. We were pretty tied up. I had it on vibrate and I forgot to check afterwards, sorry. If you've given it the once-over, I'm happy."

"It's only a request for information at this stage. 'Have you seen her? If she sees this, can she get in touch?'"

"Great. I need to know if the garages at the back of the row of shops on Homestead Avenue have been searched. The bins especially. John, get on to whoever is overseeing the troops. I expect they'll be pretty much done for the day, but they need to be examined urgently. It's a bit of a forlorn hope but the killer got in and out, and chances are if he got away with it once he would try it again using the same route."

"I was down there, boss. I think it was inked in for tomorrow. It's not that close and when Julie chased him, he went off down the road in front of her house."

"I know, but a lot more has happened since then and with our new information I need this done. Now, if you would, John."

Jordan rarely became impatient, and there was a hush around the room. "Sorry, John, it's just that I've got a feeling about this. Just one of those things that feel as though we were meant to find out about it."

"I'll sort it, boss. I'll get it done now."

"Good man."

49

Chapter 21

Jordan texted his wife to let her know it was going to be another Friday night on her own.

Why don't you go to your sister's? I'll try to come over there tomorrow. We'll go for a pub lunch.

She would know that the chance of a pub lunch was dependent on so much that it probably wouldn't happen. Jordan knew she would end up going with her sister and her family. She messaged him back to let him know she was staying at home and having an early night. She'd leave something in the oven for him when he got in. He was glad. The empty house at the end of a long shift was always depressing. He sent her a smiling emoji.

He rounded up Stella and John Grice, and they risked the cafeteria for a meal. It wasn't bad in the end. The pasta bake wasn't too dried out and there was a decent apple pie.

"We need some cover for this evening. There'll be feedback from the appeals, and we might hear from Pat Roach. Stella, see who's available. I'm going to look at the CCTV from the electronics shop and then answer the phones for a while, barring any further developments.

He had been at his desk for less than fifteen minutes. The background noise was mostly phone conversations. It was always the same after a media appeal and much of it would be useless, but it was an essential tool and now and then it paid dividends. The call that got the blood pumping came from one of the women in the search party behind the shops. It was late and many of the officers had finished at the end of shift, but there were always some who would stay on, even on a Friday night.

"Boss, we've been through the bins. We might have found the knife. Forensics are on the way, and we're questioning the shop staff to find out whose bin it was. Not that I think any rules apply, they all just use whatever has space. The knife was wrapped in a towel, bit gory that. It was pushed in under the black bags. Not much of an attempt was made to hide it. There is a broken mobile as well, no SIM, and it's pretty smashed up. If it was your victim's, I don't think it's going to be any help. I've had it collected and labelled. The bins should have been emptied today and I reckon the idea was that it'd be on the landfill by now, but the dates have been changed since the bank holiday. I can't believe our luck."

"That's brilliant. Thank you so much. I owe you a pint."

"Are we not on overtime then?"

"Oh yes. I'll make sure you are. But I still owe you a bevvy."

"Brill."

He finished the call and snagged his jacket from the back of the chair. "Stella, I'm off back to the shops. I know I can't do much, but I just want to be there."

"I'll hold the fort here, boss. Will you come back, or shall we see you in the morning?"

He paused and looked around at the busy desks. He should come back.

"Boss, why don't you call it a day? There's not much you can do, and we've got all the phones manned. I'll let you know if Pat Roach turns up."

"Okay. Why not? Thanks, everyone. I've ordered pizza, should be here in ten minutes. There was a muted cheer. A meal they didn't have to pay for was always welcome. See you in the morning, Stella. I'll be in early."

Chapter 22

The forensic team were suited up and wearing gloves and shoe covers. The bins had been open to everyone up until today, and the access road was filthy and littered. But there were rules. This was now a crime scene. The crime scene manager, in charge of the investigation at Julie's house, was managing the access as it was now part of the same inquiry.

"Do you need to go down there, sir? They have collected and tagged the knife and the cloth it was wrapped in, and now they are bagging up the rubbish. There's not much to see and it's not very nice. There is a safe route which may seem to be a bit of a joke under the circumstances, but we do what we can."

"No, I just wanted to come round," Jordan said. "I'll go and have a word with the bloke from the electronics shop. Have we got a house-to-house in the flats above the row?"

"Yep. Not everyone is at home, of course, but we're leaving calling cards. We would have got to this in the next couple of days, Jordan."

"I know you would, Ted. It's just that we had a bit of luck. I see they've removed the plastic crate from the tyre tracks."

"Yes, they made a mould. Got that out of the way early so our vans could come down. Mind, we are protecting it as much as we can. Now, we've got to get all this stinking rubbish down to the lab. Why can't they be nice clean bins, eh? Why is it never something with dressmakers' offcuts and buttons? Why is there always a bloody takeaway? Some of those bags really honk. Course, they delayed the rubbish collection, so it's all been sitting there getting more and more rotten."

"That's a good point. I reckon the person who dumped that knife thought it would have been taken by now and didn't realise about the rescheduling."

"There you go, something for you to ponder, eh?"

Jordan gave a huff of a laugh. "Yeah, because I haven't got enough to 'ponder'." He made air quotes with his fingers.

"Keeps the old grey matter ticking over. I'll get on. I'll let you know if anything unexpected happens."

"Right, get me on my mobile."

Jordan turned and walked the length of the narrow road and down the front of the shops to the property at the end. Although it was closing time, there were lights still on in the retail units and people huddled together watching and gossiping. A blue car pulled into the entrance to the garages. The driver argued with the uniformed officer at the turn-in. She was firm and with a juicy expletive, the driver reversed into the main road, wheels spinning and the tyres sending loose gravel flying. The officer pulled out her notebook and made a performance of noting the registration. Flicking two fingers at her, the driver sped away. It was a minor incident and Jordan didn't imagine that the driver was anything other than an ignorant, entitled prat. He wouldn't be drawing attention to himself if he knew what the force was doing at this relatively quiet location, in such large numbers, on a Friday night when there was much more activity elsewhere in the city.

Chapter 23

The owner of the electronics shop sat behind his counter fiddling with a phone. The cover was off, and he was poking at the innards with a couple of probes. He glanced up as

Jordan entered. "Oh aye, reckoned you'd be back when I saw all that todoment. What's happened now, then?"

"We've made a discovery in the rubbish bins outside. I wondered if you ever had a look at that video footage."

"Had a quick scan of it. Saw a couple of cars, some kids on bikes, nothing out of the ordinary. There's always people stuffing things in the bins, there's mattresses of course and tyres and all sorts of junk. It's a free-for-all. I've said they should be locked, but it's a waste of time. Bloke from the council said I should train my cameras on 'em. I told him to bugger off. What would be the point, they wouldn't do nothing anyway. There's no proper lighting either."

"It was the early hours we were interested in. We have a witness who says she saw some suspicious activity on Friday morning."

"Aye, that's right. I saw that. I suppose it was suspicious in hindsight. It wasn't a good view though. All I could see was the rear of the car, the taillights and one wheel. It was a hatchback, dark-coloured. I couldn't see the number plate if that's what you were going to ask. It's obvious somebody got in, then they buggered off. Your people might be able to enhance it. I possibly could if I had the time but it's not my job, is it?"

"No, that's right. I'm grateful for the help you've given us so far."

"Aye, well, don't go spreading that around." It was obvious from his grin that the comment was light-hearted with no serious intent. "Was there anything else?"

"No, you might be bothered by my people in the next day or so. We have to make sure that this character wasn't someone who lives here but I have to say that is looking unlikely. There is just one thing though."

"Aye?"

"The flats above this block, are they occupied by shop owners or rented separately?"

"Mixed. The takeaway family rent all their unit and live upstairs. The girl in the nail bar uses all of her set-up, but I think the rest of the flats are just renters; separate, like. We all pay the same landlord. He must be making a packet, but to be fair, he's decent. The rents aren't outrageous, and he does some maintenance."

"Have you been here a long time, then?" Jordan asked.

"More than ten years."

"You must have seen some changes."

"Aye, some. Not as much as you might imagine though. We're a bit of a backwater really. There used to be a butcher, and a greengrocer, but the supermarkets have seen them off. We still have the bakers. They do a nice steak pie."

"And the residents upstairs? I suppose they change quite regularly."

"Oh, aye, constant swap over. Take the one over my place. Two different tenants this year alone. Mind you, I think the one that's got it now might have done a flit. I haven't seen hide nor hair of him for a couple of weeks. A bloke on his own. They can be a bit unreliable, I reckon. Not like a family. I wouldn't be a landlord. Wouldn't mind the money but couldn't be doing with the hassle."

"Do you know anything about him? The chap upstairs."

"Not much. Seen him going up to the flat. Youngish, probably twenties maybe thirties. Just average."

Chapter 24

Penny was delighted when Jordan walked in with a bag from Nando's and a six-pack of beer.

"This is a nice surprise."

"I feel a bit guilty but there're plenty of people manning the phones and they know how to reach me, and

I'll go in early tomorrow. Things have stalled a bit from my end, so I thought I'd take advantage."

It wasn't such a lovely surprise to either of them when the phone rang just an hour later. Jordan glanced at the screen and grimaced. Penny lowered the volume on the music player.

"It's Stella. I thought a Saturday night off was too good to be true," Jordan said.

"We've had a sighting of Pat Roach, boss. I thought you'd want a heads-up."

"Excellent. What do we know?"

"Guard on the Blackpool train recognized her. He noticed her because she was on her own among all the hen parties and stags. She got into a bit of a row with a couple of girls who were the worse for wear on drink and kicked her bag or something. Anyway, she got off at the station in the town centre. I've been on to the local police and have requested CCTV from the railway. I'm waiting for that now."

"We can't do much unless we pick her up on the street cameras. We can hardly go wandering around Blackpool on the off chance we might see her, especially not on a Saturday night. Is anyone still in the office, apart from you?"

"The night shift answering the calls and the usual shift blokes. The fingertip search and house-to-house are finished for today. I was on to the lab earlier and they have put a hurry-up on the knife. To be honest, though, boss, what are the chances of the right size and shape of blade and in the same area, chucked in a bin just by coincidence?"

"You're right, we've found our murder weapon. I'm a bit torn now. I could come in just on the off chance that she's picked up in Blackpool. There's stuff for me to do."

"The Blackpool nick has got our contact details. If she's seen, they'll let us know right away. I've told them that she's not a suspect and we just need to have a word. We'd just be kicking our heels."

"Yes. But I think we're going to the seaside tomorrow."

"Great stuff. I'll pack my bucket and spade," Stella said.

"I've just seen the weather forecast. I reckon a Sou'wester and wellies would be wiser."

"Always rains when I go to Blackpool. We used to spend hours in the amusement arcades."

"Hopefully there'll be more for us to do tomorrow than throw away our money on slots."

"So, are we going to ask them to contact her, or do you want us to do that?"

"If they find out where she is, I'd rather do it ourselves," Jordan said. "We don't know that she's done anything, and I don't want to cause a fuss if she's just having herself a few days away."

"Bit odd when her friend has just been killed though, eh?"

"It certainly is. I'll pick you up in the morning, at about six. Unless you want to go in your environmental protection."

"No, you're all right," Stella said. "If this all comes to nothing, you can drive me through the Illuminations."

"Oh right. I've never seen those."

"You're kidding me."

"No. Why would I?" Jordan said. "Blackpool was in the frozen North when I was a kid. Ha, still is but now so am I."

"Your Harry would love them. Maybe not quite yet but give him another couple of years and you have to take him. It's magic for kids."

"Well, if the worst comes to the worst and we don't find Pat Roach that'll be something to look forward to anyway."

Chapter 25

"Do you know the way?" Stella asked.

"Roughly. Could you program the satnav or your phone?"

"No need, I know the way. When you get to Switch Island, take the M58." They joined the motorway which was still relatively quiet, and Stella unscrewed the top of a thermos of coffee. "There you go, boss, I've got some bacon and egg butties if you want one."

"Oh yes please, you're a gem. This is starting to feel like a day trip. I reckon you're right, I will have to take Harry and Penny. Shame about the weather just now." It had started to drizzle and fine rain coated the windscreen as the wet road started to sing under the tyres. "I hate this on the motorway, the spray is filthy, and visibility is terrible. Okay, to business. Although this sandwich is ace."

"Here, have the other one. We need the next junction on the M6. That'll be a bit busier so probably not the best idea to eat and drive but I won't tell anyone if you don't."

"Fair enough. Have we had anything back from the Lancashire Constabulary?"

"They've got plenty of CCTV as you expect but like everywhere they are short of bods to view it. The DS I spoke to was arranging for some of the civilians coming in today to focus on it and he'll keep us informed. We need Junction 32 and then the M55. That'll get us into town, then head for West Division Headquarters on Clifton Road. Junction 4, turn right and then left. DS Mark Bolland said it was after the Tesco Extra. He'll meet us there. More coffee?"

"Always, and I don't suppose there's another sandwich?"

"Another butty coming up. You can get the fish and chips later if we get to go see the lights."

"You're on."

* * *

The Lancashire Constabulary building was new and impressive. "I thought there was no money for anything," Stella said.

"I'm sure someone justified it. Makes our place look a bit shabby. Where are we meeting this DS?"

"I have to text him, and he'll come and take us in. He said that might be better than us wandering around, lost."

DS Bolland was tall and well-built. His dark blond hair was cut short at the sides. The top was gelled and styled. He wore a dark blue suit and a striped tie that probably belonged to a sports club or school.

He stretched out his hand to Jordan and nodded at Stella. "You found us okay then?"

"No problem," Stella said.

"Been here before, sir?" He addressed the comment to Jordan.

"No. But DS May knows Blackpool quite well."

"Yeah. It's always been popular with hen parties and the like. Cheap thrills and all that. Gives us plenty of work. Of course, I'm not local. Moved up from the Home Counties a year or so ago. I live out in Lytham St Annes. It's not bad there, for now. It was always the better end of town. It'll do until I can move back down south. If you want to come this way, we can get you fixed up with a coffee, then I'll show you what we've got so far. I reckon I've found your missing woman."

"Excellent. We're okay for a drink. We'd rather get on."

"Right, if you're sure. We can head straight down and have a look."

The room was full of desks with screens. As they entered, DS Bolland marched across to a workstation in the corner. A young woman swivelled her chair around and pushed it backwards half a metre. Mark Bolland moved behind her and put his hands on her shoulders. They saw her shrug and lean forward.

"Do you want to grab a couple of chairs from over there, DS May?" He indicated a group of chairs that had been used for a meeting.

"We'll use these," Jordan said, as he leaned to an empty desk and pulled two seats towards them.

"As you like," Bolland said.

He grabbed the back of the technician's seat and rocked it slightly from side to side until she planted her feet flat on the floor and tensed her legs. He laughed and leaned down towards the civilian. "So, Sue here is the one who spotted your woman. We picked her up outside the station and then followed her down into town."

"Was she on her own?" Jordan asked. He was looking directly at the woman.

Bolland responded. "Yes, on her own all the way."

"Perhaps we could have a look?" Stella said.

"Of course." The technician scooted her chair forward and clicked the keyboard. "We had the picture from your people and a very good description of her. We knew which train to watch for. This was one of the easier ones really. The train was full of groups, many of them party types. A couple of families. She stood out a bit, being on her own at that time of night."

As she spoke, she fast-forwarded the footage. They watched Pat Roach scurry along the road. A couple of times she moved out of the way of groups who took up the width of the pavement. Now and then she glanced up at the flashing lights. At one point, she stood for a moment to watch a tram pass by, music blaring and colours beaming into the night.

"I see what you say about the Illuminations, Stella. I had no idea."

"Oh yes. World famous for good reason," Sue said. "Now, I thought this was interesting."

She zoomed in on the figure standing at the pavement edge. Pat Roach had taken out her phone and was swiping at the little screen. After a short while, she turned and carried on walking, holding the phone in front of her. "Looks to me as though she's following directions."

"I think you're right," Jordan said.

"She seems to know which way she's heading and walks straight to the hotel." As she spoke, the technician let the video run on and then paused as Pat Roach climbed the three steps to a bay-fronted house with a hotel sign in the window. There was another sign showing 'No Vacancies'. The woman knocked once and then pushed open the front door.

"She doesn't come out again so she must have already booked a room," she said.

"Excellent work, Sue," Stella told her.

"Thanks. I'm glad I could find her for you."

Jordan copied the address into his phone. "Has she come out again today?"

"Haven't seen her and I've been through everything we've got through the night and up to about..." She glanced at the time stamp on the screen. "Half an hour ago."

"We'd better be off then," Stella said. "Need to be there before there's a chance for her to leave."

"Do you want backup, Detective Inspector?" Bolland said.

"No, you're all right. We've no reason to arrest her at this point. We just need a word. Thanks so much, Sue. Great work," Jordan said.

When Bolland escorted them back to the car park it was still drizzling rain. A cold wind was coming from the sea. "Will we see you again today?"

"We'll call in on the way back and let you know how things have gone. Thanks so much for the help."

Bolland shook Jordan's hand and turned to stomp away as they went into the inhospitable weather.

Jordan plipped the key.

"Sorry, Jordan, I think I'd better use the toilet," Stella said. "Sorry."

"It's okay. I'll pull the car round and meet you by the door."

The automatic doors swished quietly open. Bolland was leaning against the reception desk talking to a uniformed officer. "Copy Lane have their quotas covered. Bitches and Blacks, I hope they've got a couple of gays just to make up the set."

The older officer looked up as Stella walked past and had the decency to blush. Bolland lifted his chin to stare straight at her and gave a slow and deliberate wink before laughing and turning away.

Chapter 26

"Do you want to drive while I let the team know what's happened?" Jordan said. "I've got the directions up on my phone; it's not far."

"Yeah, fine."

"Are you okay?"

"Yes. I'm great," Stella said. "Let's get on with this and get out of here."

"Hey, what's going on?"

"Oh, it's nothing. Take no notice of me. I'm just being a daft mare."

"Have I upset you?"

"No. Not you, and I shouldn't be getting in a strop, it's ridiculous."

As she spoke, Stella pulled out of the car park and into the traffic. She drove for a while with just the Google voice and the swish of the wiper blades. Her knuckles were white as she gripped the steering wheel.

They drove towards the seafront. The sun began to burn through and light glinted on grey water and low surf. They could smell the sea, but there was the heavy aroma of frying food, hot dogs, and burned sugar. The strings of lights and plastic, moulded figures hanging from lampposts and above the road, looked tacky in the weak morning light. They could see a pier ahead of them and the tower looming over the town.

"I guess it looks better at night," Jordan said.

"Yeah, and possibly when you're sixteen or bevvied. It's way past its heyday, I guess. Sad really, and I think I was happier with my memories. We weren't wild parties and drunks, Jordan. We were just kids having a good time. We would come on the bus, go to the pleasure beach, go on the rides, have some fish and chips and a couple of drinks and then, if we had the time and the money, we'd maybe go to a club."

"Hey, you don't have to justify yourself to me. What is wrong, Stel?"

"I just felt that DS Bolland made out we were all just daft drunks. I know there's plenty of that goes on, but he gave the impression that everybody coming here is the same. It used to be better. It used to be the only chance the workers from the mills and factories had for some fresh air and a bit of a break. Oh, I know that's years and years ago but my nan and granda came here for their honeymoon. Granda still talks about it as something special. I just thought he was being a bit – well, a bit stuck-up and snotty about the people who come here and the North in general."

"He's a berk, Stel. It's obvious he's a misogynist and a snob."

"Yeah, and that's not all."

"How do you mean?"

"Never mind. I'll tell you about it later. This is the place we're looking for."

The road was lined with buildings declaring themselves hotels. Many of them were still trying – bay windows were backed by swagged curtains, there was clean paintwork, wooden garden tables and chairs with bright umbrellas. Many were down at heel, shabby, and a great many were boarded up and falling into ruin.

"God, this is dead depressing. I haven't been for ages. I hadn't thought about how long until now. I knew it was struggling but it's horrible," Stella said.

"I guess the pandemic did for a lot of them. Maybe they'll recover now. Look, that's the one," Jordan said.

They parked in front on the double yellow lines.

"If we get a ticket, we'll refer them to DS Bolland," Jordan said.

Stella didn't laugh. By the time Jordan climbed out of the car she was already walking up the steps to knock on the door.

Chapter 27

The door opened into a hallway redolent with the smell of bacon and toast. The floor was laminate, and the walls were cream wallpaper. One was covered by a huge seascape. It was clearly not the Irish Sea and Jordan doubted very much that blond, tanned surfers in bright shorts often walked along the grey sands. A bell had chimed as they entered, and now a young woman appeared behind a desk across the corner near the stairs.

"Good morning, you're very early. Have you got a reservation? Only, check-in isn't until three."

Jordan had his warrant card in his hand and introduced himself.

"We haven't called the police. Least I don't think so. Mrs Chalmers might have. Hang on, I'll bring her," the girl said.

"No. We're not answering a call. We just need to have a word with one of your guests," Stella said.

"Oh."

They waited for her to ask for a name, but after a few beats, Jordan was the one to speak. "Ms Roach. Pat."

The girl shook her head.

"Sorry, is Ms Roach not with you?" Jordan asked.

Again, a shake of the head. The girl's face was red, and she pressed her lips tightly together.

"Is something wrong?" Stella asked.

"Can't," the girl blurted.

"Sorry?"

"I can't say anything. It's forbidden. Mrs Chalmers will have my guts for garters. She says, no matter what, Lisa, no matter what, we do not give out information on our guests. So, can't. I'd lose my job."

"I see," Jordan said. "Tell you what, why don't we have a word with the owner."

"Can't."

"But you just said, you'd fetch her. Mrs Chalmers."

"She's not the owner. She's the landlady, though she's supposed to be called the manager. Mr Chalmers is the owner. He's away. Don't ask me where, I can't tell you. Not allowed."

Jordan ran his hand over his face. "Okay, Lisa – it is Lisa, isn't it?"

The girl thought for a moment and then nodded her head.

"Okay, great. Tell you what, why don't you either let us have a glance at your register" – he pointed at the heavy book on the countertop and Lisa's eyes widened as she slammed it shut – "or, why don't we have a chat with the erm, the manager."

"Right. Right. Just a minute please."

The girl picked up the handset on a landline and jabbed at the buttons. They waited until she informed the elusive Mrs Chalmers that there were two coppers in reception, that they wanted personal information, and she really hadn't said anything at all to them, nothing, but please would she come through as quick as possible because she was out of her depth.

Jordan didn't dare glance at Stella who had turned away and was studying the seascape with great attention.

The door behind the counter opened and a slender woman came through. Her grey hair was neatly trimmed. She was dressed in a cream dress and jacket. "What's going on, Lisa?" she said, glancing at Jordan and Stella.

Jordan thought it might save time if he got in the first words. He flashed his warrant card. "We need to speak to a woman who we believe is a guest at your hotel."

"I told them, Gran, er sorry, Mrs Chalmers. I told them I couldn't say anything."

"Oh, for heaven's sake, Lisa, use your nous. They're detectives. If they say they need to speak to someone, then they do and it's no good messing about, they'll do it anyway. Sorry about this, Detective Carr. Lisa, go and help with the breakfasts."

The girl turned and scurried towards the door. "And wash your hands first."

"Yes, Gran. Oh sorry."

"Never mind. Just go." The woman turned back and shook her head. She shrugged. "What can you do? I used to have a nice French girl on reception. Juliette, come to improve her English. A couple of girls to do the rooms and help with food, Lithuanians. Lovely girls. All gone.

Bloody Brexit. Then the lockdowns and the pandemic nearly finished us off. We got the loans and things we were entitled to, did some refurbishing. We even opened the dining room for that eat-out nonsense, but it's been hard. We're hanging on, just. We have another place that we've turned over to a hostel. Asylum seekers. They have to go somewhere and it's regular money, but we're trying to keep this a proper holiday hotel. I don't know how we'll manage if we don't have a good season with the lights and then the Christmas break. This time next year we might well be gone. Generations my family have been hoteliers in Blackpool and now what have we got, empty places all up and down and bloody Lisa. She might be my granddaughter but… Oh well, never mind. Now then what can I do for you?"

Jordan had taken out his phone and opened the image of Pat Roach. "We need to have a word with this lady, do you recognize her?"

Mrs Chalmers nodded. "Mrs Booth, came yesterday." As she spoke, she opened the register and turned it towards them. She pointed to the entry. Mrs J Booth and Paul Booth. There was an address in Surrey.

"Are they still here?" Jordan asked.

She glanced at a rack behind her. "Yes, the key's not here."

"Could you call their room?" Stella pointed at the phone.

"Hold on," Mrs Chalmers said.

They could hear the ringtone sounding out. They waited until it became obvious that there was going to be no response.

"They're not in the dining room," Mrs Chalmers said. "There's just a couple of builders in there and a little group of lady pensioners. They could have gone out and not handed the key in. They're not supposed to. Fire precautions. If there's a fire, we need to know which rooms are occupied. People don't understand. They think it'll save them time."

"Maybe we could go up and have a look?" Jordan said.

"Yes, but I'm not that keen on opening the door if they're not there. It'll come back on me if anything goes missing."

"We are the police," Stella said.

"Yes, that's true. Well, okay then."

The room door was unlocked. It was no surprise to any of them to find the cupboards and drawers empty. There were two wet towels in the bathroom and the covers on the beds had been roughly thrown across the mattresses. The key was on top of the dresser.

"Done a bunk," Stella said.

"Looks like it. Mind you they were only booked for one night and they paid up front."

"Did they use a card?" Stella asked.

"No, he paid with cash. It still happens sometimes. We have some oldies who've been coming for years and it's how they like to do it, so we haven't gone to card only. Mind, I did think it was odd because he was younger. I'm sorry."

"We have been watching on CCTV and she wasn't seen leaving this morning. Do you have a back door?" Jordan asked.

"We do, but it's the fire exit. The alarm would go off if someone opened it who shouldn't. Oh, just a minute." She went to the top of the stairs and yelled down. All pretence of the professional landlady was lost as she bellowed to the floor below. "Lisa, get yourself up here now, girl."

They heard the thunder of feet on the stairs. "Lisa, have you let anyone out of the back door today?"

"I did, Gran. Mrs Booth and the man with her. I knew they'd already paid, and they said their car was out the back. I was being helpful, like you say, going the extra mile." The girl smiled at them. Pleased with herself.

Chapter 28

Lisa hadn't seen which way the couple had gone, she didn't know where the car had been parked, or indeed the make or colour. She was confused and a little disappointed that her grandmother didn't applaud her effort.

On the way back to Lancashire Constabulary headquarters Jordan asked again what it was that had annoyed Stella, and after a short hesitation she told him about Mark Bolland's comments overheard in the reception area.

"I don't know why you're surprised," Jordan said. "It was obvious from very early on what he was."

"Why aren't you annoyed, though? We could report him."

"Not a lot of point, to be honest. We have enough on our plates right now and sometimes you just have to suck it up."

"No."

Jordan blinked in surprise. "Come on, Stel. We've seen it before, and it'll happen again."

"But that's the problem. If we suck it up, then people like him just go on and on. They get into places where they should be changing things, they don't and it's a lost cause."

"I know, I do know. Jesus, Stel, I'm fully aware of prejudice, I've dealt with it all my life. When I was a kid, I was written off by so many people. My dad was dead. My mother was effectively a single mum. Black family, three lads and a girl, a lone parent. People made assumptions. But it wasn't like that. My mum was tough, and she wouldn't stand for any nonsense. We had Nana Gloria who was unshakeable. She made us rise above it and in doing that we won. We've all done okay and we're all happy. It's better to prove yourself rather than try to bring down others. Then, when we are in the position where we can make a difference, we start to fix things."

"Yes, I know what you're saying, mate, I do. But to be honest I can't agree with you."

"It's up to you, of course. If you want to put in a complaint, I'll back you to the hilt."

"Well, let's see how we go," Stella said. "We might well not even have to see much of him again. I'm going to have a word with that Sue though. I'm going to let her know I saw what I saw and if she has problems with him, I'm an ally."

"Fair enough."

They didn't bother to let Bolland know they were in the station. They went straight to find Sue who was just on her way back from a break.

"I didn't see your woman leave. I watched all the time," she said.

"We have a time for when they left, but not much more. They went out of the back entrance. It's an alleyway so there'll be no traffic cameras. I don't know what you'll be able to find for us. We have very little information. We assume they went to a car but even that is open to doubt," Jordan said.

"Can you give me a bit of time? I don't work well under scrutiny. The break room has a coffee machine, but the cafeteria is pretty good if you want to eat."

"How the other half live, eh, boss," Stella said.

"Yeah, it's great here. I love it, love my job," Sue said.

"You don't want to take the next step then?" Jordan asked.

"How do you mean?"

"Join the force."

"I've thought about it but there's stuff that doesn't sit well with me."

"How so?" Stella asked.

"I guess I could just say, *the establishment*. Let me put it this way. If I want to leave and go somewhere else, it's just a change of job. If I join the force and then leave, there's a lot more for me to lose. I'd be a failure, in many eyes. The pension is important, and an ex-copper is always an ex-copper."

"Isn't that a good thing?" Jordan said.

"Is it? Well maybe and then sometimes it's not. Anyway, I've decided I can do a lot of good where I am, and I'm happy with that for now. Why don't you guys go and grab a sandwich or something and I'll see if I can find anything of any use?"

Chapter 29

They ate a quick lunch. There was a good selection of hot and cold food, but Stella took a salad and Jordan had a sandwich. Neither of them was in the mood for a leisurely meal. There was work to be done. Jordan spoke with John Grice. He updated him and told him that Pat Roach had a companion and they were using another name, at least on occasion.

Nothing exciting was happening back at Copy Lane. The team had been sifting through messages from the appeals. Now that Pat Roach had been found – and lost – they were ready to put all of those on the back burner and try to trace the car from the lock-up behind the shops.

"It's not the same car, is it, boss?" Grice asked.

"It's a hatchback, it's dark blue. Get on to the digital department, they could be able to give us a make by now. Send me a text as soon as you have it. My feeling is not but we need to know for sure."

"I did wonder about that," Stella said. "But you think not?"

"The car by the shops had two blokes in it. There has been no mention of another bloke and why would Roach come on the train if there had been a car available? It doesn't seem right to me."

As they walked back into the squad room, Sue raised her hand and beckoned to them. "I might have something for you," she said.

"Really? Damn it, you're good at this, aren't you?" Jordan said and was rewarded with a beaming smile.

"We do what we can. Anyway, I was able to access a camera on the corner of that back alleyway. It's an off-licence so they have coverage. There was a car emerging at about the right time. There was only that one for over half an hour so, by my reckoning, that has to be yours. There are two people inside, look." She pointed at a still in the corner of the screen and Jordan and Stella leaned in.

"Okay, guys, what's going on?" Bolland said as he marched across the room. He dragged off his jacket and threw it onto an empty chair. "I was in a meeting. Nobody told me you were back. What mischief has Sue been up to?"

"She's been a great help. We're very impressed," Jordan said.

"Oh, we do what we can." Bolland echoed the other woman's words.

"Well, Sue has," Stella snapped.

"All right, love, take a breath," Bolland said.

"Detective Sergeant May is quite correct," Jordan said. He turned to look directly at Bolland. "We are in the middle of things here, so if there wasn't anything?"

"Boss, here's the car," Stella said. "That certainly looks like Pat Roach in the front passenger seat." She turned to Sue. "Are you able to follow her?"

"For quite a way, yes," she said. "They go along the front and then back into another alleyway down by the tower and vanish. I'm still trying to pick them up again."

The group gathered around the screen. Sue glanced at them all, a frown creasing the skin of her forehead.

"Let's give her some room, eh?" Jordan said. "Can you put the images onto another monitor for us?"

"Hold on. These are from ten minutes ago." Sue clicked some buttons and the large screen on the wall lit with the scene of the car travelling northwards.

Several other officers and staff glanced up.

"It's all right, you lot get on with what you're doing," Bolland snapped.

Stella had already picked up the number plate and was searching the ANPR records. "The plates don't match the car, boss," she said.

"Okay, stolen I expect," Jordan said. "She is certainly making herself more and more interesting. Have you got any patrols down by the tower who could be on the lookout for that?" He addressed this to Bolland, who was looking like a spare part.

"Yes, I'll get on it."

"I've done that, sir," Sue said. "Two cars in the vicinity and they are already alerted and heading that way."

"Brilliant. You can have a job in my team anytime, Sue."

"Does that go for me too? I taught her all she knows," Bolland said with a grin.

"Not so much, thanks," Jordan said. "Come on, Stella, let's get down there."

A murmur travelled around the room and there were a couple of quiet sniggers.

"I'll use the Airwaves to keep you updated," Sue said.

"You really are a gem. Thank you so much," Jordan said as they ran for the exit and the car park.

Chapter 30

"I'll say one thing, boss. You can make a point when you need to," Stella said as they turned out of the car park and back towards the seafront.

"Don't know what you mean," Jordan said, but a grin lifted the corners of his mouth.

"Did you see his face? 'Not so much' – that was brilliant."

"I just answered his question," Jordan said.

"Yeah right. Well, I thought it was ace."

"I reckon we can use the blue lights. Probably a bit out of line, we're on foreign ground but I don't think anyone is going to say anything." As he spoke, Jordan pulled into the middle of the road and turned on his integral flashing lights.

They straddled the white line as traffic moved out of their way. One or two of the drivers flipped a finger at them. Pedestrians watched them pass, but everyone moved. They sped past the tower and the war memorial. Sue was directing them using Airwaves radio.

"Down there," Stella said as she pointed into a narrow turn.

They could see the patrol cars parked diagonally across the alleyway. The officers were peering into the windows of a blue Vauxhall.

"Gone," one of them said as Stella and Jordan joined them. "Sorry. They were off before we had chance to stop them. PC Clerk gave it a go, but it was a lost cause, they had a head start. They went off into the main road and got lost in the crowd." The officer pointed to the end of the alley. "We've been in touch with headquarters. We gave them a description such as it was. A man and a woman. He was in jeans and a dark jacket. She had trousers on and a long green coat. She had a bag, like a big handbag thing. Long strap." He pointed to a pair of wedge heel sandals thrown aside. "She was keen to get away. Left her shoes. Do we need to have CSI down for these?"

"Bag them and tag them, will you? Tape off the car and keep an eye on it. This is a developing situation. Thanks for your effort, lads," Jordan said.

"Just wish we could have grabbed the buggers," the older officer said. "What have they been up to?"

"Well, that's the thing," Stella said. "To be honest, we're not sure yet. The longer this goes on, the more it seems that it's something dead dodgy. They're certainly digging a big hole for themselves, given this started with us just wanting a chat."

"Well, sorry to break it to you but I'd say they weren't up for a bit of a natter."

"No, I think you're right," Stella said.

Jordan and Stella walked to the main road.

"It wasn't the same car, Stel. I've had a text from John. The one in Liverpool was a Ford. They haven't been able to enhance the number plate."

"So, what do we do now, boss?" Stella said.

"They're on foot. We get a BOLO out to bus and railway stations. We alert all patrols and hope they're spotted. Will they head back to Liverpool or try and go somewhere else? If so, where? Right now, we don't have a clue. We know who Pat Roach is, but we don't know about her mate. She was supposed to be a friend of Julie Scott. That looks less and less likely as time goes on but what does that mean?"

"Unless she's just scared," Stella said.

"Scared?"

"Yeah. Maybe she knows something about what happened to Julie, and she's just scared that she's at risk."

"But why would she run from us? Could be fear, or did she have something to do with Julie's death? At the moment, either could be the case. I think we have to hang around here for the time being. If they're still in Blackpool, we can't just head off back to Liverpool. If they leave, we are at least better placed to be after them. With luck, we'll pick them up here."

"Back to their headquarters?" Stella asked. "I'm not sure how welcome we might be with Bolland."

"Don't care about that," Jordan said. "But we'll have a drive around first. I don't hold out a lot of hope that we'll spot them, but you never know. I'll get their car taken back to Liverpool. It'll cost a bit, but I want to be in charge of what happens to it. So, you drive. I'll have a word with DCI Lewis and get that organised."

Jordan walked back to where the patrol officers were taping off the area around the car. "I don't want any interference with this. I'm going to have it taken back to the pound. I might want my team to examine it at some stage. No offence but they already have some DNA and so on. Can you guys stay here for now? Sorry, I know that's a bit of a pain."

"You're all right, Detective Inspector. We'll get a coffee from the place on the corner. We're about to go off shift. Any chance there'll be overtime?" the older one said.

"I'll do what I can. Appreciate your help."

"What's it all about, anyway? We were just told to grab 'em if we could."

"We've got a dead body on our patch. These two might be involved. That's the size of it at the moment. The longer they run the more determined we are to have a word."

"Fair enough. Mind you, there's a lot of ways they can go from here. The Lakes, the Dales, if they get to Lancaster and Heysham they can get to the Isle of Man. These are all places where they can get lost easily. There're not many cameras in the hills. If you don't find 'em soon, they're in the wind."

"You're not making me feel any better," Jordan said.

The officer laughed. "Telling it like it is, that's me, eh, Pete?"

"Yeah, it's being so cheerful that keeps him going," the younger man said.

"Well, I hope your mates are on the ball," Jordan said.

"They'll need to be lucky. Needle in a haystack as it gets later. The crowds will be coming in for the lights and it's a bit mad then. Good luck with it, mate. Right, Pete, mine's a cappuccino with chocolate sprinkles and see if they have any KitKats."

Chapter 31

They drove around for a while as the sky darkened and traffic coming into town began to build. The seafront was lined with cars moving slowly through the Illuminations. The pavements thronged with families, groups and couples. There was litter everywhere, and as time passed, the atmosphere became more and more raucous.

They could hear reports coming in over the radio. Now and again, there was a possible sighting, but they all turned out to be innocent couples out for an evening.

"Back to the headquarters, I suppose," Jordan said. "I don't think we're going to get our fish and chips at this rate, Stel."

"To be honest I've gone off the idea. Been smelling them all day and it's got me craving a salad."

They drove back to the seafront. The direction of traffic was in their favour now with the majority of cars entering from the Lytham end and driving down past the tower and out towards Fleetwood.

"We've seen them." Sue's voice over the radio was urgent and excited. "They've boarded a train at Blackpool North. On the way to Lancaster."

"Okay, we're on our way in. We need to alert the Transport Police. Are there cameras on the train?"

"DS Bolland is on that now, sir."

By the time they arrived at the station, there was a general buzz. This was more interesting than picking up drunks and pickpockets. Mark Bolland was at a desk alongside Sue. He turned as Jordan and Stella came into the room. "First stop is Poulton-le-Fylde. We have them on camera." He pointed at his screen.

"That's her," Jordan said.

"Okay. Do you want to speak to the Transport Police?"

"I'd better."

The officer from the Transport Section was calm and relaxed. Jordan assumed some of his attitude must come from knowing that no one could escape until the train stopped and they opened the doors.

"Are we arresting these two?" He wanted to know.

"No. We would like them to come in voluntarily, but it doesn't look as though they want to do that. We'll have to bring them in to question them under caution. Have you somewhere to hold them while we come through?"

"No, it'd be better if we bring 'em back to you. We'll escort them on the next train to Blackpool. Do you expect them to kick up rusty?"

"I hope not. Make it clear that we just need a word and that we'll take care of them. If they are running scared, which is a possibility, we can protect them."

"Okay, we'll do what we can. I'll let you know when they're on the train. It'll be about an hour. You've time for a cuppa and a pie."

Chapter 32

They were both tired, but a couple of cups of strong coffee and a piece of apple pie for Jordan and an Eccles cake for Stella pumped them up with caffeine and sugar.

One of the younger uniformed officers came into the canteen looking for them. "Your suspects are about to arrive at Blackpool North. Two cars are there to pick them up, DS Bolland wanted to know where you want them."

"Have you got any interview rooms that aren't too grim?" Jordan asked.

"None of the rooms are that bad, to be honest. Haven't had time for the bozos to screw them up yet, though it's not for the want of trying. We have a couple that could be called lounges."

"Great, can we put them in there? Keep them separate, though they have had plenty of time to confer and get their stories sorted. If that's the way they are going to go."

* * *

Pat Roach looked travel-stained and nervous. She had been given a cup holding a brown drink. As there was no smell of coffee, it was probably tea. No matter, it was on the table untouched.

Jordan carried a file and his tablet PC. There was nothing in the file but a couple of blank pages and a map of Blackpool. However, it looked official.

"Ms Roach, are you all right?" Stella pulled out one of the chairs and smiled as she slid onto the seat.

"No. I'm not. Why would I be all right? What the hell is happening here? I've been chased by the police, dragged off a train and now you want to know if I'm all right." She looked as though she might cry.

"We only want to ask you a couple of questions. About your friend, Julie. You know what happened to her?"

"Of course I know about Julie. How would I not know about her? Why do you think I legged it?"

"That's exactly what we wanted to ask you about, Ms Roach. May I call you Pat?" Jordan said.

"I suppose. Am I in some sort of trouble here? Why have you done all this? Am I under arrest? Do I need a solicitor?"

"No. You're not under arrest. This should have been explained to you. We want to interview you under caution." Jordan went through the routine. "You do not have to say anything, but it may harm your defence if you do not mention something when questioned that you later rely on in court. Anything you do say may be given in evidence. Is that okay? Do you understand?"

"No. It's not okay, and that sounds like I'm under arrest. I do need a lawyer, don't I?"

"It's up to you. If you want a solicitor, just say so and we'll arrange it. But, Pat, there is very possibly no need for that. It will just slow things down."

"Okay. Where's Paul?"

"He's in another room. We'll have a word with him in a while. Why did you leave Liverpool, Pat?"

The woman didn't answer immediately. She reached for the drink and turned the cup round and round on the table. Some of the cold liquid inside splashed onto her hand and she wiped it away with a fingertip. She raised her eyes to glance between Stella and Jordan.

"I was scared. Shit-scared, if you must know."

"What were you scared of, Pat?" Stella said.

"What do you think? My mate has just been killed."

"Yes. I can see how that was horrible and upsetting for you, but why scared? Scared enough to leave in a car that we believe was stolen?"

"No, no that car is Paul's. He got it from a mate, that's all I know about that."

"Who is he, Pat? Who is Paul?"

"He's her son, isn't he? It's Julie's son."

"We didn't know Julie had a son. We spoke to her before she died and to her mother afterwards. Nobody mentioned a son," Jordan said.

"No. Well, they wouldn't, would they?"

"Why not?"

"Listen. He was just helping me out. He hasn't done nothing. I didn't mean to get him into trouble."

Chapter 33

They left Pat Roach snivelling into a paper tissue, watched over by a female officer. They had offered her food which she refused, but she was sipping at a large takeaway cup of cola. "Be nice to him," she said. "He's not a bad lad. He's had a rotten deal. He's a bit fragile."

Fragile Paul was in another room. He had pushed the chairs apart so that he could stretch out his legs. An empty plate and the smell of onions in the room said burger and fries.

"Okay, Paul," Jordan said. "First of all, is it Paul Scott? You had no identification. No driver's license, nothing."

"I don't have to have. What is this, effing Russia? Anyway, no, it's bloody not. Haven't been Paul Scott for yonks. It's Palmer. My dad's mum was Palmer. Why would I want to have my dad's name? He didn't want me, so I didn't want him. She wrote to me though, till she died. Nanny Palmer, the only family I had."

"You didn't have a bank card. That's odd these days. Can we look at your phone?"

"No, you can't. I've not had it long. My other one was cancelled. This is just a pay-as-you-go and I need it. I'm changing my address. All that stuff is on hold till I'm settled."

"Okay. Let's get this sorted out, shall we, and then we can all get on our way? Have you been told your rights, and do you understand them? I am going to record this if you're happy with that."

"Fill your boots, mate. Whatever. I'll have another drink, though."

Jordan nodded to the constable standing by the door.

"Another Irn-Bru is it?" the bobby said.

"Unless you can stretch to a beer."

"We can't do that, I'm afraid," Jordan said. "Hopefully, we can get you on your way before the pubs shut, though."

"I don't know what you want me here for. What do you think I've done? I haven't done nothing. I gave Pat a lift. She wanted to get away from the Pool. She was upset."

"Where were you going, Paul?"

"Yorkshire. Well, we was until your mates chased us."

"Why did you run away if you hadn't done anything wrong?" Stella said.

Paul turned and looked at her now. He stared for a couple of minutes, raised his eyebrows, and rubbed his chin with his thumb and forefinger.

"Well?" she repeated.

"Pat said she wanted a ride. I gave her a ride. You'll have to ask her why. All I was doing was helping her out. I wasn't running away. I was helping a mate."

"Why did you change the plates on your car, Paul?" Jordan asked.

"Pat said she didn't want anyone to know where we was going."

"Didn't you think that was a bit odd?" Stella said.

"Yeah, I did a bit, but I reckoned if she wanted to tell me then she would. Otherwise, it was none of my business."

"Very trusting of you," Stella said.

"She was good to me when I was a kid. So, I helped her out. You've got those cameras everywhere, you'd have picked us up in no time so I had a word with a mate. It's not that big of a deal."

"It's illegal," Jordan said.

"Aye well, you'll have to fine me then, won't you."

"So, you met Pat here in Blackpool, did you?" Stella said.

"Yes. Well, obviously."

"And you stayed the night in the hotel?"

"Yes."

"In one room?"

"How do you mean?"

"You and Pat stayed in the same room in the hotel?" Jordan said.

"What are you saying? What the hell do you mean?"

"Nothing. She's a fair bit older than you, isn't she?"

"So, what's wrong with that?"

"I'm not saying there's anything wrong with it. It just seems a bit odd to me. I wouldn't want to do that, would you, Detective Sergeant? Sharing a room with someone you don't know that well."

"God no," Stella said. "That's well weird."

"It had two beds," Paul said. "We just slept there. You dirty sods. What are you saying? We couldn't afford two rooms. We just slept in two beds. Anyway, I knew her when I was a kid. We used to sleep in the same room sometimes then."

"Okay. How did you arrange to meet?"

"Do you know what?" Paul said. "I'm not saying anything else. I don't want to answer any more questions. I'm leaving. I've had enough of this. I haven't done nothing wrong. I've told you. Tell Pat to give me a bell when she decides what she wants to do. Where's my car? They said you'd got it."

"It's probably in the pound by now," Jordan said.

"What!? Oh, for God's sake. You're winding me up. You're not serious. Why would you do that? Why the hell would you do that?"

"We didn't know what was going on with you. There's been a murder. We felt we may need to examine your car. It had false plates."

"What am I supposed to do now? I don't know about any murder, do I?"

"We can offer you a bed for the night. In one of the cells?"

"You have to be effing kidding me. Aw, man. I don't believe this. This is last, this is. When can I have it back? I need my car."

"Well, you help us, Paul, and we'll do what we can to get you back on the road as soon as possible. We'll search your car, and you answer our questions. The quickest way for you to get out of here is to help us."

"No, you can't search my car. You've no right to do that. I haven't done nothing wrong. Jesus, this is well out of order. You can't do that. I'm sure you can't. I'll have you for this. I've got contacts."

"Is that a threat, Paul?" Jordan said. "It sounded like a threat to me. What do you think, Sergeant?"

"Oh yes, boss," Stella said. "That was deffo a threat."

Paul Palmer stared at them both for a minute, then lowered his head to the table and covered it with his forearms.

"Bloody Pat. Bloody soddin' hell," he said.

Chapter 34

Paul Palmer didn't want a solicitor even after he was told he wouldn't have to pay for it. He didn't want anything more to eat or drink. He picked at his fingernails and refused to speak.

"Okay, we're getting nowhere with this. We'll leave you for now until I have a word with my boss and we decide what is going to happen. You're not helping yourself here, Paul," Jordan said.

There was no response.

In the other room, Pat Roach had her head on the top of her folded arms laid across the table. There was the faint sound of snoring. She jerked awake when the door closed behind Stella.

"Where's your mucka?" Pat asked.

"Busy," Stella said.

"Can I go?"

"You can go at any time, but we have some more questions for you. We would prefer it if you stayed."

The other woman shrugged. "You couldn't get us a cuppa?"

"Of course. Just tell the constable what you want. Do you want some toast, a sandwich?"

"No. Just a drink and I want to go. Where's Paul? Is he waiting for me?"

"He's still here. He's not being very helpful. What is it with you two?"

"How do you mean?"

"To be honest it seems a bit odd. I mean you're a lot older than he is, and yet you shared a room in the hotel. We know that. He told us."

"So?"

"Well, just between us, that's a bit odd."

"I've known him for a long time. There was nothing to it. I know what you're hinting at, and it's bollocks. God, as if. He's like my own son."

"How's that then? You said he was your mate's son."

"He was if you count just carrying for him nine months as important. There's more to being a mum than just being pregnant."

"Surely that's all there is to it? She had him, he was her son."

"She didn't want him. She didn't care about him. Think about it, she didn't even tell you about having a son. She hadn't seen him for years. She'd moved on. Nobody knew about that part of her life. She was only with Paul's dad for a few months, and it was never happy."

"Well, okay, so how come you know him so well?"

"It's a long story."

"We have plenty of time. Why don't you tell me about it?"

"I knew him when he was little. Julie didn't want him. His dad was away on the rigs and his nan wasn't interested; his other nana had died by then. They only got married because she got knocked up and it was never going to last. Poor Paul, he was never welcome."

"That doesn't tell me how you knew him?"

"When they split, Roger moved away, following the work for a long time. He took the baby with him because she was going to give him up for adoption. But he was away at work so much, it was so difficult. He couldn't really do it on his own. That's when I first met him. He was on the rigs, and I was working up north. Okay, we had a bit of a thing for a while. Some of the time he was fostered out or with childminders, when his dad was away. But we saw him regular. I even had him to stay now and again, when it fitted in. I had my own lad with me then, so they were company for each other. They were only very little. The social services wouldn't have approved, but I figured what they don't know won't hurt them. We got on all right, and I treated him well. I just gave him a bit of love. Anyway, when me and Roger split, I kept up with where he was. I couldn't have him anymore and then I was homeless for a bit and could barely look after myself."

"Okay. So how come you were friends with Julie? That's a bit weird. You knowing her hubby and then making friends with her. Everything about this is a bit peculiar."

"It's not really. I can see how you'd think that but sometimes things just happen, don't they? I came back to Liverpool. This is where I was born. That was the main thing me and Roger had in common. He'd lived in Aintree, well Netherton really. They moved to Old Roan when they were together, him and Julie. We had stuff in common. Us Scousers, you know, we have a bond. When we split, I came home. Anyway, I was nosey, couldn't help myself. I wanted to know what she was like. I found where she lived – not hard. Roger had talked about it enough. When the job came up where she worked, it was too good to be true. Meant to be, I reckoned. I was still in touch with Paul, and I decided I wanted to tell him about his mam. I wish I hadn't now. I just thought it'd make me look clever. Maybe I thought it would paint me in a good light. After I left his dad, Roger badmouthed me a bit. It's complicated. I cared what he thought about me. Anyway, it was as I say, I did get on with her. I liked her. I never expected that we'd be mates. We shouldn't ever have been. I should have disliked her, I suppose. I didn't. I just didn't."

At this point, Pat wiped away tears which had leaked from her eyes and tracked down her cheeks. She sniffed. "You'll think I'm mad, but I thought I could, you know, get them together. I thought Paul might meet her. They might like each other. It was a bit doolally I suppose, but in the end, it never worked out. He never met her. I was going to do it after the holidays. I was going to get them together. Not going to happen now though, is it?"

There was quiet until Pat spoke again. "I was wrong, okay, I know I was wrong. I was scared. I thought they could come for me next."

"Why?" Stella said. "Why would you think that?"

"I don't know. I just don't know. She was my friend. She was dead in the most horrible way. Paul gave me a lift and we were going away until you lot had sorted it. That's all."

"What about your own son?"

"Oh, he's grown up now, moved on. They do, don't they?"

"Maybe," Stella said.

Chapter 35

Jordan was finishing a phone call at the desk he'd been assigned when Stella came back to the incident room.

"I've had a long chat with Pat Roach," she said. "It's all a bit of a mess, but actually I think I believe much of it. She was trying to do some sort of peace-making or some *Long Lost Family* thing – like on the telly. I honestly don't know what to make of her. I'm not convinced about her reasons for running away. I mean, okay, her friend has been killed, but why has she, well, overreacted – I reckon that's it, overreaction. She's pretty cut up about it all, that's true. What are you thinking about Palmer?"

Jordan shook his head. "Nothing I can pin down, but there's a lot about it that's dodgy. His lack of ID for a start, a pay-as-you-go phone, the number plates on his car. He's not talking anyway now."

"According to Pat, he didn't know his mum at all. He was really little, a baby, when they moved away. Then he was fostered, sometimes in care. It's a familiar story. Nobody but Pat seemed to care about him," Stella said.

"I wonder if that's true. Trouble is we don't have enough for a warrant to look through his phone or search his car; although the registration anomaly means we can hang on to that. I haven't anything to hold him on. We're going to have to let them go. We can try and persuade Pat to go back to Liverpool and offer her protection but if she doesn't want to, we can't force her," Jordan said.

They let them go. Jordan tried to persuade Pat to go back to her home, but in the end, the best they could do was take their phone numbers, and ask them to keep themselves available if they needed to be talked to again. They asked them not to leave the country. With no proof of wrongdoing, even that was nothing more than a request.

"Have they had a chance to examine his car?" Stella asked.

"I tried to get the bloke at the pound here to do something but there was no chance to do much more than just a quick visual examination, which turned up nothing. It's so bloody frustrating. It doesn't add up to me. We'll have the car taken back to Liverpool and get our team to have a look. He refused a DNA swab. We told him that doesn't look good, but he wasn't having it. He seems pretty clued up on his rights. Is that because we've had dealings with him before?"

"That's a good point," Stella said.

"There's something here and I just can't shake it loose."

"Do we have any idea where they're going now?"

"No. With no car they'll be on public transport unless they hire something. He's got no license though, so it would have to be from somewhere dodgy. I don't think there is anything more we can do with them. I will see if we can have a block put on them leaving the country as persons of interest. I don't know whether I'll be able to swing it with DCI Lewis, but it might be worthwhile. We'll ask the guys here to keep an eye on dodgy car dealers and monitor the bus and train stations. I guess we might as well head back to Liverpool."

DS Bolland offered to find them somewhere to stay. "Get you fixed up with a room, no problem," he said. "Mates' rates."

"I reckon we'll head back," Jordan said.

As they headed for the motorway Stella gave a short laugh. "God, can you imagine the gossip if we'd stayed the night in Blackpool. Life wouldn't be worth living. It was bad enough when we first started working together. All that innuendo and nudge nudge stuff going on. A night in a hotel would put the rumour mill into overdrive."

"I hadn't thought about that. I just wanted to get home, but you're right," Jordan said.

His phone rang and he poked at the keyboard to FaceTime John Grice. "We reckon we've found the car from by the garages, boss – oh, hi, Stel. It's a Ford, dark blue, hatchback of the right style, so the right age. It's burned out in a car park on an industrial estate in Kirkby."

"Brilliant. What's the situation right now?" Jordan asked.

"We've forensics on the way. I've requisitioned footage from cameras on the route from Old Roan and that's about all for the moment."

"Excellent work. Send us the directions and we'll meet you there," Jordan said.

"Did you get to see the Illuminations?"

"Seen more of them than we wanted to, honestly."

"Is Pat Roach being brought back?"

"Nope," Jordan said. "Didn't have enough to hold her or Paul Palmer."

"Who's that?"

"I'll fill you in when we come back but in the meantime are Kath or Vi still there?"

"They are."

"Brilliant. I'm sending you details, and I want all we can find on him. He was in care, fostered, and generally passed around the social services system. I want to know where he's been, what he's been doing – everything. Oh yes, he's possibly got a car registered in his name as well. Maybe not, mind you. He's definitely dodgy."

"On it, boss. See you in an hour or so."

Chapter 36

It began to rain as they left Blackpool; a cold, misty drizzle. The last sight they had of the Irish Sea was grey, the horizon smothered in gloomy cloud, and sluggish waves nudging onto wet sand. Jordan was disappointed. Not only had the chase been effectively fruitless, the place that had been presented to him as a jolly, sparkly destination for him and his family sometime in the future had turned out to be dirty, down at heel and depressing.

He felt sorry for Stella. As they turned towards the M55 she sighed. "You should never go back, should you? I haven't been here for years, and it was always so much fun in my mind. Okay, it was chavvy, I knew that, but now it's just grim and struggling. It's no wonder people go off to Spain. I mean, okay, even in those places there're fish and chip shops and cheap booze and drunkenness but there's also sunshine and blue sea. What a shame. On top of that, there's bloody Mark sodding Bolland. I'm still not sure what to do about him.

"I had a word with that civilian, Sue Clarke. She says he's a pest and everyone knows it. But they just keep out of his way. None of them wants to risk causing a fuss. I told her that if she wanted to report him, to let me know.

She said she probably wouldn't because, after all, it's just him being a pig. It's not right."

"It's not. Maybe now you've drawn attention to it, now she knows it's so obvious, she'll think about it."

"But what about you?"

"Me?" Jordan said.

"Yeah, that racist comment I told you about."

"Oh, that. Nothing new and in fairness, I didn't hear it myself, did I? No, that's going nowhere. I reckon it's best ignored."

"Bloody hell. What a shitshow this is all turning into," Stella said. "You disappoint me."

"Hey, come on, mate. We're still working on Julie's murder, and we'll get there. This case is still very much live, so let's just concentrate on the things we can do something about, yeah?"

She didn't respond but stared out at the wet road and the rush of traffic through the spray. Jordan saw when she wiped away tears of frustration. He didn't mention it.

As they joined the busier M6, her head leaned against the window. Now and again, she snorted in her sleep.

* * *

Stella yawned, shivered, and dragged her coat tightly around her as they climbed out of the car in Kirkby. There was crime scene tape across the entrance to the car park. They could see very quickly that the vehicle was completely destroyed. The air was thick with the smell of burned rubber and melted plastic. White-suited figures bent and crouched around the shell which was little more than scorched metal and broken glass.

"We're getting nothing from this," Jordan said.

"Nope, but we've got CCTV and there are cameras all over the place here. We might see who did this."

"Yes. Good to see you're feeling more positive."

"Sorry," Stella said. "I was just tired and hungry."

"We really should get something to eat. Tell you what, let's have a word with John, a quick chat with the forensic sergeant, and then I'll treat you to those fish and chips. That's unless you want a salad."

"You're on. Fish and chips, and a pint of lager."

Chapter 37

John Grice was waiting beside the burned-out hulk. The collar of his Puffa jacket was turned up and a beanie hat sat low over his ears. "It's a dead loss, boss. They really did a number on it. We'll have it taken in. But the forensic guys have all been standing around shaking their heads and sucking their teeth."

"What have we got?" Jordan said. "There's always something."

"Yeah, that's true. There was nothing in the boot. There are no bodies, but you'll have guessed that already by the lack of that particular circus. There has definitely been use of an accelerant. The doors were left open. So, it looks as though they probably sprayed or poured the fire starter inside and then tossed a flame in there. It's all very usual. With a bit of luck, they might have scorched their eyebrows. I have put out an alert to the local hossies in case anyone turns up with burns."

"Good man. So, our best bet is to see them on the CCTV."

"It's already been requested. At least we know when they came here. A bloke in the houses at the back called the brigade at around five. I had a listen to the recording of the call. He said he'd been watching the telly and became aware of the weird light and then smelled the burning. He knew straight off what it was. As you know, it's not that unusual around here. He didn't even look out. He said he didn't want to open the door and let the stink in. His garden fence is too high for him to see the car park without coming out of his living room. He got on the blower and then walked around from the front road. By that time there was a crowd of kids on bikes. He kept the stupid sods back, so they didn't get fried. But he didn't see anyone running away or what have you."

"We'll do a house-to-house at those residences overlooking the car park. You never know, we could be lucky." In the flicker of light from the emergency vehicles, he saw Grice raise his eyebrows at the thought that any of the local residents would want to become involved with the police.

"Yeah, I know. Also, we will probably need to have a word with any local kids that have been into this stuff before."

"That's a fairish list, boss."

"I know, realistically, we can hold that until we've had a look at CCTV. Listen, did Kath and Vi get on to the search for Paul Palmer?"

"They were hard at it when I left but it was end of shift. They might still be there, but I haven't heard anything from them. I asked for a report to be sent to us all if they came up with something interesting."

"Okay. I guess that's it until we get the CCTV footage. We're going to go and get some fish and chips and a bevvy. Do you fancy it? I can fill you in on what happened in Blackpool."

"Great stuff. Oh yeah, before I forget. The DCI was looking for you earlier. He wants an update in the morning. There's a gold team meeting at nine and obviously, he wants you there. Says he's been putting them off for long enough – his words, not mine. He said he had tried to ring you in Blackpool but got no answer."

"Shit. I put my phone on silent while we were interviewing. Right, I need to make sure my book's up to date, you lot as well. Though I'll assume they are."

Grice nodded, but Stella turned from gazing at the fire brigade who were packing up their equipment.

"I'll do it tonight. It's okay, but I'll just double-check everything," she said.

"Thanks, guys. I already know I'm in for a rollicking for buggering off to Blackpool."

"You didn't have a lot of choice, boss," Stella said.

"You know that, and I know that but he's going to be all, 'You're supposed to be directing things. It's your job to allocate tasks and keep control.' He's right, of course, he is. But sometimes the pressures on the ground..." He paused. "Preaching to the choir, aren't I? Oh well, that's for tomorrow; for now let's go and eat. I'm starving."

* * *

The chips were hot and freshly made, the batter on the cod was crispy and the beer was perfect. It was warm in the pub, and Jordan felt himself unwinding for the first time in days.

"I reckon we've done all we can for today. I'm absolutely whacked," he said. "I'm going to aim for seven o'clock in the morning. We need to find the blokes from the car as a matter of urgency. At the very least, we need to be able to discount them."

"Do you really think that, boss?" Grice said. "We're almost certain it was them behind the shops and didn't that young woman say she saw one of them come over the fence?"

"Yeah, I know that's what we think right now. But would you go back to a place where you'd left a dead body when you had to know the chances were that the police were still there? It's a common idea that murderers always revisit the scene, but that's not as often as people think.

Usually they are keeping their heads down somewhere far away. Unless it's a family affair and they can't run."

"Well, this isn't that," Grice said.

"I think we should try to keep a very open mind and not get hung up on one aspect of this. Have you heard anything from Kath or Vi? I haven't had a message."

"Hold on." Grice clicked the buttons on his phone. As he did, there was a chime and the sound of a phone vibrating on the table. "Ha, speak of the devil," Grice said. "They are both signing off for the night but there's a report on the way."

Jordan looked at his screen. 'Pretty successful', Vi's message said, and she finished the short message with a smiley face emoticon.

"Right, well now I've got some bedtime reading on top of everything else," Jordan said. "I'm off. See you in the morning. Thanks, guys."

Chapter 38

Jordan was awake before the sun, he spent the quiet hours checking his notes for the meeting with the gold team. Ready for work he stuck his head around the bedroom door where Penny was reading to Harry in bed. "Might be late, love. Sorry."

Penny smiled. "We'll be here, don't worry."

Leaving them in the warm house Jordan had a moment of unaccountable fear. Would she always be so accepting? Would his boy ever hold it against him that he was so often at work?

* * *

As he walked down the corridor in the Copy Lane station, he could smell coffee. Stella looked up from her screen as he entered and raised her mug in greeting.

He poured himself a drink. "Did you read the report?"

"Yes. They did a good job. Palmer had a pretty unstable upbringing. I argued with Pat Roach when she told me that Julie didn't become his mother just because of biology and there was more than that involved. I have to say though having read about the way he was shuffled around and passed from pillar to post, I am having to reconsider my stance. I don't understand it. Okay, I'm not a mam, but I just don't think I could ever turn my back on any child that I had. You read all the time about women who had their kids taken away and they spend decades trying to find them and yet she could have had him with her. She had family to help and everything. Even her own mam, his granny, seems to have washed her hands of him."

"I haven't made any decisions about it all yet," Jordan said, "but there are plenty of people who have difficult childhoods, and they don't go wrong. Although quite a number do. We'll work through it and stay as open-minded as we can. First of all, though, I've got that meeting. I want you and John to go and take the picture of those blokes from the car to Old Roan and take an image of Paul Palmer. Speak to both witnesses and see if they can recognise any of them. Fingers crossed. Also, I'd like Kath to arrange for us to speak to Palmer's dad. Tell her to get in touch with the company that runs the oil rig. Find out if he's there now and if so whether we can have a video call with him. If he's at home on the Wirral, we'll go over there."

"Okay. But what's the idea behind that?"

"Just background. I'm covering all the angles."

* * *

97

Gil Lamb looked more together than when Stella had last seen her. She'd had a good weekend, she said. Her husband had been at home to help.

"We won't keep you long. Can you look at these pictures and see if you recognise the men in them?"

Gil studied the printouts carefully. She carried them to the window to examine them in a better light. In the end, she turned and pursed her lips, shook her head. "I'm sorry. I can't say for certain. These are pictures inside the car, they are blokes sitting down and although they are not very clear they are close-ups of their heads. I only saw one of them. I can't be sure. I'm sorry."

"It's okay. It's not your fault," Stella said.

"The thing is, I had more of an impression of him than a proper look. It was dark and he was moving fairly fast."

They showed her a picture of Paul Palmer. "What about this man?"

Again, she gave it plenty of time but couldn't identify him as the man she had seen. Stella tried not to let the disappointment show.

They took the pictures to the manager of the electronics shop. "I dunno, mate," he said to John Grice. "Can't say one way or the other."

"But the car is the same one," Grice said.

"Might be. Yes, could very likely be. But if I was to have to put money on it, I wouldn't say for sure that those blokes were the same as I saw the other night. It's just two blokes in a car, end of."

"Well, that wasn't a lot of use," Stella said.

"No, if anything it has made things even more confusing."

The reaction at the station was the same. They tossed around ideas and thoughts, but with no definitive identification, they were back where they started which wasn't very far at all.

"I want to see the CCTV footage myself," Jordan said later. "Not because I think I can do it better," he reassured the team. "I just think maybe looking at it might spark an idea. I don't mind if anyone with time goes through it again. Any ideas would be welcome."

Chapter 39

The call from the forensic department came mid-morning. Jordan had just poured himself coffee and stood by the window stretching his back after hours studying the CCTV footage. It wasn't his job. Kath and Vi would have made notes on everything they had seen, but he wanted to look at the men who had been seen near the garages. He needed to watch what coverage they had of the car before it had been burned out in the car park.

"That was the lab," he told the team. "They found prints and DNA on the knife from the bins. Swabs have gone away for analysis. Julie's blood has been matched, but apart from that the rest of the evidence is logged and noted. No matches have been found on the databases. We all know how long this stuff takes, so for now we just work with what we've got."

He went back to his desk to stare at the images on the screen. At the earlier meeting with the gold team, he had been upbeat and given the impression that they were moving forward. Sitting in the incident room right now, he felt frustrated and had to acknowledge, even after everything they had done, nothing had brought them the breakthrough they so desperately needed.

On-screen, the car drove through the streets around Old Roan. It sped away from Homestead Avenue. They picked it up a few times until it went under the A59 and then disappeared into the residential conglomeration with the racecourse on one side and the M57 on the other. It had been Kath widening the search who had picked it up two hours later in Kirkby. He made a mental note to compliment her on her work and make sure it was noted in her records.

The offices and warehouses on the trading estate all had decent coverage with cameras. But the car had been driven onto a patch of grass away from the buildings before it was torched. He noted the names on the various units and handed the information over to the two women. "Make sure we've taken footage from all of these places. These blokes must have had someone to pick them up, surely. Which way did they go when they left the car?

"I think we've got everything there is. We haven't viewed it all yet, there're hours and hours. The main thing was that we found the car," Vi said.

"Absolutely. I'll allocate reviewing to a couple of the civilians. They'll liaise with you."

"These blokes could have gone over the railings, boss. Somebody might have picked them up on the main road," Vi said. "They might have legged it into the housing estate. I suppose it's possible they had another vehicle hidden. That suggests a great deal of preplanning. It's a needle in a haystack. We'll keep trying, but we need some luck."

"I'm keen for us to do this. With footage of them running away, Gil Lamb might have her memory jolted if she sees them moving," Jordan said. "We need to either confirm this is the same men who were seen leaving near where Julie was killed and whether or not it was Paul Palmer."

"Oh, right. That makes sense." Kath clicked a couple of buttons on her machine, stretched her arms above her head, tensed her shoulders, and then leaned in again to watch the film of not much happening on her screen.

There was a call from the family liaison officer soon after lunch. Julie's mother wanted to know when the body might be released. She wanted to begin to arrange a funeral. "She's getting distressed about it," the officer told

Jordan. "She's old and pretty much on her own now. She's fretting about all the stuff she'll have to do. She's worrying about the house. She's fussing about bank accounts, and Julie's will; all sorts of things. Poor old thing spends a lot of time sitting on her own and just going over and over what's happening."

"What has she said about a will?" Jordan asked.

"She is convinced Julie had made one. With her job as a financial advisor, it was something she was particular about, by all accounts. She'd helped her mum to make one."

"Leave it with me. Tell her I'll try and get an interim certificate so we can release the body. I'll pop in there to see her this afternoon and have a word."

After he finished the call Jordan sent a message to John Grice telling him to contact Julie's office and see if anyone there knew about a will. "Try her bank as well, and I'll find out if she had a solicitor when I speak to her mum." He sent a message asking the evidence officer if one had been found in the house. There would be days of work sorting her things, but if they had an idea what they needed to look for it could only help.

He walked down to the digital forensic section. "I need to speak to whoever is dealing with Julie Scott's electronics."

The man on reception scrolled with his mouse. "Okay, it's not allocated yet."

"Really? Well, how long before someone has a look?"

"Could be a while. We're backed up as usual. Nobody put a rush on this."

"Okay. I want to ask for a rush on her computer."

The officer scrolled. "No, no computer."

"How do you mean? I need a report on her stored documents. I need to know if she had a will on there."

"There is no computer. There's no phone either."

"So, what do you have?"

"A clapped-out tablet that's so slow it'd be quicker to write a letter, and a fairly new Kindle. Not that much, to be honest. Less than we would expect."

Jordan spun on his heels. "There must be a mistake here. I'll look into it."

"It could have been a cock-up with the evidence officer. I have to say it's unusual but not unknown. Anyway, if you find it, I'll need paperwork to rush it through."

Jordan bit his tongue and stormed up the corridor to the evidence room. There was no record of it. He insisted on going through the paperwork and in the end even the boxes of stuff that were labelled and bagged and it just wasn't there.

"Stel. Meet me in the car park. I want to go and have a word with Julie's mum."

"Okay, on the way, but, boss…"

"Yes."

"We've been able to arrange a Zoom call with Paul Palmer's dad over on the rig."

"When?"

"Two hours."

"Well, you'd better get a move on then, eh?"

Chapter 40

Doris Beetham looked unwell. She had lost weight in the short time since Jordan had last seen her. Her fingers shook as she pulled a green cardigan around her body. The liaison officer was with her and disappeared into the kitchen to put the kettle on. "Coffee is it, Doris?"

"I don't care, love. Just anything." She turned to Jordan and Stella who had taken off their jackets and sat opposite her on the brown settee. "I hope you've brought me some good news, lad," she said.

"I'm working on it, Mrs Beetham. I'm trying to get you what we call an interim certificate. It'll mean that you can bring Julie home and have a funeral."

"How long is that going to be?"

"I can't say exactly, but honestly I'll do everything I can to speed it along."

"But you still haven't caught the evil swine that killed her?"

"We're doing everything possible. I have a great team and we're putting in all the hours that we can. But we don't have anything positive to tell you yet. I will make sure you know as soon as we do. Is there anything else I can do?"

"Like what?" The old woman sighed and turned away brushing at the moisture in her eyes.

"What about family? Is there no one who can come and keep you company? You must be awfully lonely dealing with this on your own."

"There's nobody."

"What about your ex-son-in-law?"

"Don't be daft. I haven't seen that no-mark for years. He was as much use as a chocolate fireguard even when he was around and that wasn't for long."

"What about your grandson?" Jordan knew he was pushing the issue and it was a clumsy attempt, but he was aware of the time and the interview which was just over an hour away.

"Paul? Is that who you mean?"

Jordan nodded. Doris Beetham sniffed and pulled a handkerchief from her cardigan sleeve. "One of the biggest mistakes I ever made, Paul."

"How's that?"

"I could have tried harder. I could have kept in touch."

"Why didn't you?"

"Julie. It was all my Julie. She wasn't well after he was born. Her marriage, such as it was, was falling apart. She never said, but I think that Roger was a bit free with his fists. All she wanted was to get rid of him. Never should have married him in the first place, but she didn't want to be a single mum. She'd have been better off. We all would. He wouldn't go without the boy, and in the end, she came round to mine one day and just told me he'd gone. I was heartbroken. He was such a lovely little lad. She said she couldn't cope and that it was better if he went with his dad. I begged her to tell me where he was at first, but she wouldn't have it and time went on and it sort of drifted away. I'll be honest, she went a bit loopy for a bit. I was very worried about some of the stuff she was doing, but after a while, she did all right. She dropped all the daft stuff, went back to college, got herself a proper job and she was good to me. I could never understand how a mum could do that, just give up her babbie, but she was my daughter and I had to stand by her."

"What was the 'daft stuff'?" Jordan asked.

"Oh, talking to fortune tellers, having her palm read. It was like she was looking for something. I think it was all part of her depression, to be honest, and it stopped eventually. I was just glad it was over, and she never talked about it again."

"I understand she had made a will."

"Oh that. It's just one of the things I'm fretting about. I know she wrote one out. She had a neighbour witness it and that Pat Roach, I think. She helped me to do one. There was no need, really. Everything I have, which isn't much – I don't even own this place – was to go to her. I don't know what happens now. People like me don't do wills. What have we got to leave? But she said if I didn't, everything might go to those bloody criminals in the government. So, I did it. Now it's made things worse. If she's left her house and her money to someone, then I'll probably need to change mine. Then again, maybe I don't need to. I don't know, do I? It's all beyond me."

"Did she have a solicitor?" Stella asked.

"No. I don't think so. She downloaded some forms from the internet."

"Where are they? Do you know?" Jordan asked.

"Mine is here. In a box in the sideboard. I don't know where hers is. She said she was keeping it on her computer, she'd kept a copy of mine as well, but I wanted to have one I could hold in my hand. They're not real otherwise. I don't know about her, but haven't your people found it? Can I not go and look around her house? I need to go and clean up anyway."

"We can arrange it for you," Stella told her "You don't want to have to do that, Mrs Beetham. Let us sort that for you. DI Carr has asked the forensic people to look for the will. If there was one in the house, then they'll find it."

"I'd be grateful. I have to say I wasn't looking forward to going. I don't think I'll ever be able to go there again."

"You don't need to do anything you don't want to. You have to look after yourself," Jordan said.

"You're a good lad. Are you married?"

"I am, and I have a little boy."

"That's nice. It's a hard job you do. Thankless, I bet."

"It can be. But let us help you to sort things out and if you need anything else just tell the liaison officer and she'll get a message to me or DS May. Just one last thing, did Julie have a computer at home. I'm sure she had one at work, but did she have one in her house?"

"Oh yes, one of the folding ones. It was usually in the living room, on the little table by the couch."

When they left her, Doris was wiping at yet more tears, but she seemed calmer.

"That's all a bit peculiar, isn't it?" Stella said.

"About the fortune tellers and what have you?"

"Yeah."

"Well, I'm not sure. I mean look at that old woman you visit, the cake woman."

"Betsy. Yeah, but she's old and she's got something."

"How do you mean, 'got something'?" Jordan said.

"She knows stuff. I don't know how and it's true that a lot of it can be explained away but..." Stella shrugged.

"Well, yes, it's all a bit peculiar and it could just be that she was going through a hard time but it's background, so it's useful. The more we know about her the better. I'm still finding it hard to settle on a main hypothesis. We have to consider a robbery gone wrong. She said nothing was taken with the first break-in. She did disturb him so was it the same bloke coming back? They'd made such a mess I don't think there can have been much to take really. Except..."

"Yeah?"

"Her computer," Jordan said.

"Didn't she say it was dodgy?"

"Yes, she did, but even so, where was it? It hasn't been found in the house, it's not in evidence, unless there's been a cock-up."

"Perhaps she'd stuffed it away somewhere unlikely. I'll get on to the evidence officer and ask him to have another look." Stella made a note on her phone.

"If it wasn't a robbery it has to be personal. Someone who knew her. Someone who held a grudge. Or someone who wanted something from her, maybe. I'm leaning towards that, but she didn't seem to know many people. There was no boyfriend that we know of. There's the ex-husband but he wasn't on the scene by all accounts."

"That brings us back to Pat Roach and Paul Palmer, doesn't it?" Stella said.

"I certainly haven't discounted them yet."

Chapter 41

The connection with the platform out in the North Sea was surprisingly good. Roger Scott sat in a small cabin. There were pictures stuck on the wall and a shelf holding a few novels and a couple of *Dungeons & Dragons* figures behind him. His face was tanned by the wind and his thick hair was streaked with grey. He was handsome in a rugged way and fit-looking. Jordan was surprised that his Scouse accent was faint with just a few giveaway terms betraying his origins.

"I don't know what you think I'll be able to tell you," he said. "I haven't seen that divvy for years. When I left, I left for good. She was one sandwich short of a picnic. If I'd known, I never would have married her. Well, there was the baby, but that was all a mistake and we'd have been better off if she'd got rid. Wouldn't hear of it though so we ended up deep in the shit. I did my best for him, but he was never any good. Okay, I had to go away for work, no choice, if it hadn't been for the rigs, it'd have been boats. I wasn't meant to stay in one place. I had no choice but to put him into care. He got fostered. I tried to keep up with him, I was with Pat for a little while and she was good to him, but she wasn't his mother, was she? Anyway, that all went pear-shaped. He stayed up in the North for a while and I saw him now and then, but he was off the rails by the time he was sixteen and he just took himself away and never got in touch. I feel guilty when I think about it. I meant to do right by him, but I know I didn't. What can you do?"

Jordan didn't respond to the rhetorical question. There were plenty of things that could have been done to stop yet another young man slipping through the cracks into trouble.

"You never thought of trying to get him to go and live with his mum, or his granny?" Jordan said.

"Those two balm pots. No. She was away with the fairies, that Julie."

"How do you mean?"

"Oh, she was doolally. First, it was religion. That's why she wouldn't have an abortion. Then it was spirits. Went to see mediums and what have you, talking to the dead for Pete's sake. What a load of crap. Then it was magic. It was just one thing after the other. Some of it put the wind up me, to be honest. Some of the books she had and some of the stuff in the house. Cards and candles and even a bloody crystal ball and some sort of bowl for spying."

"Scrying?"

"Oh, aye that was it. I suppose you would know about that sort of thing."

"How do you mean?"

"No offence, mate, but you know. Coming from Africa and that."

"Yeah. I come from London."

"Oh well, sorry. Anyway, between that and her being depressed and just bloody high maintenance I couldn't take it. But I wasn't leaving the boy with her. No way. Didn't make no difference in the end I suppose, but I meant well at the time."

"You know she did well," Jordan said. "Got herself a degree, a career."

"I heard. Nothing to do with me though. I was long gone by then. Fair play to her though. You still don't know who it was, who killed her? She didn't deserve that. Nobody deserves that."

"We're working on it. I have to ask where you were last Tuesday and Wednesday"

"Hang on." Roger tapped at his phone keyboard. "I was here all week, you can check easily. So, not much chance of me bumping her off, was there?"

"No. It would seem not."

"Come on, mate. Why would I after all this time? I hadn't seen her for yonks. I hardly ever thought about her."

"Okay. I think that's all for now. I may need to speak to you again."

"Fair enough. I've got nothing to hide. Shoot me a text and I'll send you my contact details. I'm home in two weeks. Back in the Wirral. All on my tod. The way I like it now. I'm done with nutty women."

Chapter 42

When Jordan came out of the interview, Kath was waiting to speak to him. She had found footage of the two men being picked up and driven away from the burning car.

"Great stuff," said Jordan. "Okay, I need whatever can be isolated of them on foot. Get on to the geeks in technical forensics and ask them to put a rush on it. Tell them the paperwork is on the way. I need to speak to Pat Roach. Do we know if she's still in Blackpool?"

"No, they saw her on the train to Liverpool and there have been lights on at her house, according to the patrol. So, I guess she's back at home now."

"And the son?"

"He wasn't with her. His car is still in the pound, he never came to collect it."

"That's odd. We're on our way to the Roach place. Going to have a word."

* * *

Pat Roach was wrapped in a towelling dressing gown, though it was in the middle of the afternoon. She rolled her eyes and groaned but pulled open the door and stepped back to allow access for Jordan and Stella.

"What the hell are you after now?" she said. "You already asked us everything. You had nothing. This is harassment. I'll make a complaint."

They'd heard the same or similar so many times before. "Put the kettle on, should I?" Stella said.

"No, you bloody shouldn't. I'm paying my taxes for you to have canteens at your offices, I'm not giving you tea as well."

"Okay then, we'll keep it short," Jordan said.

"Good. Then you can bog off and leave me in peace."

"It's a quick question about Julie."

"Go on then."

"While you were with her, were you aware of any interest she had in the paranormal, or anything like that?"

"The paranormal. What the hell are you talking about?"

"You know, spiritualism, magic, crystals."

"No. Is that all?" Pat moved towards the door.

"Don't you want to think about that for a minute?"

"You asked me, I've told you. Now, if there's nothing else."

"Where's Paul?" Stella asked.

"No idea. I left him in Blackpool. He wasn't coming back here. He said he'd had it with the Pool, nothing but trouble, he said."

"So, you're not in touch with him?"

"I said."

"Did you know that Julie had made a will?"

"A will?"

They waited in silence. Pat pulled at the belt on her dressing gown. She tucked a stray strand of hair behind her ear, and scratched at her neck. "Not sure. I mean that's personal, that sort of stuff."

"So, she never discussed a will with you?" Jordan said.

"Can't remember anything about that."

"You never witnessed one for her?"

"Why are you asking about that sort of thing? She's not even buried yet, why would that matter?"

"Just working on finding out what was going on with her. Any background we can get might help us to find out who did this horrible thing," he said.

"Well, I might have done but it was way back. Not long after we were friends. I mean, she had some papers and said she needed a signature and would I do it."

"You didn't ask what it was?"

"I don't think so. I don't remember now. I just signed it. She said it wasn't important and it wasn't anything to bother about."

"You seem to remember it quite well now," Stella said.

"Yeah, well you've reminded me, haven't you?"

"If Paul gets in touch, tell him we need to talk to him again. How long did you know his dad?" Jordan asked.

"It's hard to say. On and off for a bit."

"What does that mean?" Stella asked.

"Look, I don't want you here. I don't want to talk to you about all this. I lost my friend, and do I get any sympathy? Do I hell? All I get is hassle. Please go away and leave me alone and if you want to talk to me again you need to make an appointment."

There was no option but to leave her to stew.

"Where now, boss?" Stella said as they drove away from the house.

"Back to the station, I suppose, though it's getting late and it's pretty much end of shift. Tell you what, why don't you come back to mine? We're not going to get anything from the CCTV footage until tomorrow now. I've got some ham hocks slow cooking. I put them in before I left this morning, Nana Gloria's recipe. They're lush."

"Will that be okay with Penny?"

"Of course. You haven't seen each other for ages, and we can go through what we've got and try to make some sense of it. I'll let John Grice know."

"I thought the DCI wanted a word."

"Yes, there's that as well."

She gave a short laugh. "Okay, you're on. If you take me round to Copy Lane, I'll pick up my car."

"Why not leave it? You can have a couple of glasses of wine then and get a taxi home. I'll pick you up for work in the morning."

"Excellent."

Chapter 43

It was good to be away from the office early. Harry was already bathed and ready for bed when they arrived in Crosby. Jordan took him upstairs to read his story while Stella and Penny had a glass of wine and set the table.

It had been a while since the two women had been together and they spent the time catching up. They stuck to talk about Stella's flat decoration and the funny things Harry had done. Stella couldn't tell Penny anything much about the ongoing investigation and knew that Penny wouldn't press her. She appreciated that it had to be difficult when Jordan came home tired and preoccupied.

"Jordan's lucky having you. It's tough being a copper's wife. Not that many people can do it as well as you do," she said.

Penny blushed and turned away.

Jordan thundered back down the stairs and into the kitchen. "Right, ladies. Red or white wine?"

"Can I have a beer?" Stella said. "I just think it'll go best with ham hocks. I must give you my nan's recipe for peawack, I think you'd like that."

"Peawack – there's nothing called peawack."

"Bloody is. It's gorgeous, sticks your ribs together. I'm telling you, you'd love it."

"Well okay."

"Mind you, it's not that I've ever made it. All I can manage is cheese on toast, but I can tell you what she used to do."

* * *

Later, they sat in the dining room, the table cleared and their tablets side by side. "Tomorrow, I want to take the video of the blokes from that car and see if the witnesses recognise them when they see them in action, as it were."

"Okay. This whole thing, it's too many different strands," Stella said.

"It seems that way at the moment but we just need to keep going and it'll all come together. It always has."

They wrote lists and made a chart, but they struggled to connect any of the dots, and it was late when they called an Uber.

As he stood in the garden watching the taillights of the taxi disappear, Jordan took a moment. The air was chilly and smelled of damp soil. From somewhere, the autumn scent of burning leaves lingered. Rain from the day before had cleared and a silver moon just past full had risen in a cloudless sky. It was a beautiful evening, too nice to have a mind full of death and evil, but it was the way it was. He checked the gate at the side of the house was locked and turned to go back into the house where Penny had poured a nightcap. He still needed to update his record book and then maybe he'd have a full night's sleep. He would put a hopeful spin on things in the morning when the chat with the DCI would catch up with him. More than anything else, though, he needed to find justice for Julie.

Chapter 44

"Where first?" Stella asked.

"Old Roan," Jordan said. "I'll speak to Gil Lamb, and you go to the shop where we got the security footage. If they recognise the blokes who torched the car, that's one tiny move on."

"What does it tell us though?"

"It confirms that at least one of them was at Julie's house. I know that doesn't sound like much, but we still have a lot of CCTV footage to view and might see where the car was before they drove it away to destroy it. All these tiny bits build, and we end up with a full picture. It's what we need right now. Detail. After that, I need to pop in to see Doris Beetham again. There's an interim death certificate being issued today. I've just had a message. She can at least get in touch with someone to start arranging a funeral. If she has something concrete to think about it might help her to cope."

* * *

Gil Lamb came to the door with one of the babies cradled against her shoulder.

"Sorry to bother you again. I won't take up too much of your time," Jordan said.

"You're all right, I'm more organised than it might seem."

She sat on the settee and gently rocked her son as Jordan played the excerpts of footage to her. She asked to see some of it again. "Yeah, I reckon that's the bloke that came over the fence." She pointed to one of the figures. "He's the right height and build and he's a bit bow-legged, isn't he? It makes his foot land funny. I feel a bit stupid now, I thought he'd landed awkwardly but I don't think it was and I should have mentioned it, sorry. Of course, I can't be one hundred per cent certain, but I feel that it's him."

Jordan sat in the car reviewing overnight messages until Stella jogged back from the shops. She slid into the car and shook her head. "Sorry, boss. He said he doesn't think so, wouldn't commit himself about either of the blokes."

"Damn. I thought we had something. Still, we'll keep on looking at the video. I know it's time-consuming. Who is researching Julie's social media activity?" Jordan asked.

"A couple of the civilians. They haven't found very much apparently. She hasn't been on Facebook for a long time and hardly ever tweets. Nothing on TikTok or Instagram. Fairly typical for someone of her age, I guess. That's not ageist of me either, it's just what I've found to be true. What about these blokes with the car though?"

He told her about Gil's comment and her tentative recognition of the man who came over the fence. It was a relief to have something positive even though it was pretty minor in the great play of things.

"I keep coming back to why," Jordan said. "What was it about Julie that drew these people to her and was enough to see her killed? You met her, she was just an ordinary woman, on the face of it. Ordinary people are killed in horrible ways, we know that, but usually it's a jealous spouse or a robbery. None of that seems to be a part of this. There has to be something though."

The short drive to Doris Beetham's house was silent. They were both deep in thought. They pulled up outside the semi.

"No need for you to come in, Stella, I won't be long. Can you get on to John and ask him to have everyone in for a meeting in an hour? That'll give me time to speak to DCI Lewis first."

He gave Julie's mum the details of the interim certificate and told her she could go ahead and start to arrange things. He had copied out the contact details of a few funeral directors and the number for the registry office and jotted them down for her.

"Thanks, lad. That's kind of you, very thoughtful. My Julie used to do that sort of thing for me."

"You don't have your own computer then, Doris?"

She huffed and flapped her hand at him. "Heavens no. I wouldn't have a clue. It's not that I'm daft but I just never got into those things. It took me ages to learn how to use the text thing on the phone."

"You wouldn't know where Julie's computer is, would you?"

"Was it not at the house?"

"No. She did say that she'd been having trouble with it."

"Did she? She never said anything to me. Sorry, I don't know. Is it important?"

"It could be. We still haven't found the will that you mentioned and I'm hoping that there might have been a copy saved on her hard drive. Apart from that, it would help us a lot if we could see what she'd been up to in the time before she was killed. See who she'd been talking to and possibly even more important, who had been in touch with her."

"Oh, right. I'm sorry I just don't know. As for the will, I don't think it's that important, is it? She hasn't any family except me, and I don't expect there is much to leave, money and that. She had some bits of jewellery, but we're not rich. Will it all go to the government now?"

"I should think that, as her next of kin, you will inherit her estate. It might be best to find a solicitor. She owned her house, didn't she?"

"Yes. She only ever had a small mortgage and she told me she'd paid it off. She was so thrilled when she did that. It was a council house that she lived in with that husband of hers and when he moved out, she had the chance to buy it. I've only ever rented this one. I thought the council might move me on now I'm on my own but, up to now, I've got away with it. Oh well, better sort out a solicitor then. Can you tell me one?"

"I'm sorry, I can't do that, but the Citizens Advice people can help. Give them a call." He wrote the number of Penny's office onto the notes he'd already given her.

"I hope you find her computer. It was one of those that you can carry about, I do know that, but when we saw each other, we talked about ordinary stuff, the government, the prices in the shops, all of that, not computers and what have you. That Pat Roach might know of course. Did you ever find her?"

"We did, yes." Jordan paused. Should he tell her about her grandson? Was there any point? He thought not. He wasn't likely to come visiting his granny. "Never mind, Doris. If we can't find it, we'll manage without. Now don't forget, anything you need just call me or Stella."

He turned to leave and picked up his jacket from where he had dumped it on a chair in the corner of the room. As he moved it there was a faint clatter. He bent to retrieve what appeared to be a bundle of fabric and string. "Where did you get this, Doris?"

"What's that, love? I can't see over there."

"It looks like a little doll." Jordan felt a chill run down his back as he looked at the small thing.

"Oh, I don't know. It was on the step the other day. My neighbour brought it in. She said it was propped against the door. Bloody kids, that's all. You have it if you want. I was going to stick it in the bin."

Jordan took an evidence bag from his pocket and slid the doll into it.

"I'm going to have the liaison officer come and spend the day with you, Doris. She can help you get started on your arrangements. Is that okay?"

"Aye. That's lovely."

"You know, while you're waiting, do me a favour and if anyone comes to the door, don't answer it."

"Don't answer my door? Don't be so daft, what would people think?"

"Do it just for me, would you?"

"Oh, nobody's going to come. Nobody comes except her next door and she's at her son's for a few days. Another baby. That's four now. All right, if it'll make you happy, I'll just sit here and stare at the walls. Nothing new there."

As he climbed into the car, Jordan held up the evidence bag.

"Where did you get that?" Stella said.

"According to Doris, it was propped on her step. We need to speak to her neighbour, but she's away and I don't want to alarm the old lady. Ask Kath to trace her, see if we can find a phone number."

"It's like that other one."

"I know. Not exactly, but close enough to ring alarm bells. It's not a toy, is it? There are no pins or anything, and the clothes are not really copies of what Doris wears. It's like a weak copy. She wasn't a bit bothered, so I guess Julie never told her about the other ones."

"Don't think she had the chance, did she?" Stella said.

"That's true. Just as well, the poor woman has enough to contend with. Soon as we get back, will you take this down to the lab and see if they can find anything to connect to the other two? I'm sure they will. More CCTV feed to look for, I'm afraid. We need to know who left this and we need to protect Doris."

Chapter 45

DCI Lewis listened in silence as Jordan updated him on the latest developments. He blew out his cheeks and sighed.

"What have you done about Doris Beetham?"

"I've got the liaison officer with her right now and there're patrols passing as often as they can manage. I don't want to alarm her, but I'm worried about tonight."

"Okay. We'll have a car in the street. I don't need to tell you that we need to handle this, Jordan. We can't have a repeat of what happened with the daughter."

"I'm aware of that, sir."

"What else have you got on at the moment?"

"A hit-and-run, though I think that's pretty much sorted. Just got the paperwork to do for the CPS. There's a domestic with the husband in the wind. We've got an all-ports out for him, and John Grice is keeping a grip on it. An older case regarding two migrants found dead at the docks and I'm due in court at the end of next week."

"Okay, I'm going to have the migrant one reassigned. You need to concentrate on this case and get me some progress. This is no reflection on you, Jordan. It's complicated and confusing but the press are mumbling about no movement and it's in danger of going cold."

"We're working as hard as we can, sir."

"I appreciate that, but we need results. Soon. Let me arrange some protection for the old lady. Is this black magic?"

"I honestly don't know. We've looked into it in the city, but I can't find a proper link between Julie Scott and any of the places where this sort of thing goes on and certainly not with her mother. We do know that Julie was dabbling in spiritualism and what has been described as magic. But I don't think it was part of her life, maybe at one stage but not lately. Unless we really are missing something. I'm trying to keep all options open and that's all we can do for now, I think. We've spoken to the next-door neighbour and she found the doll on the step, propped against the door. There was no note, no one around, and there are no security cameras on any of the houses."

"Okay. Stick at it, Jordan. Keep me in the loop."

* * *

Stella called on the internal phone just as he arrived at his desk.

"I'm down in the lab, boss. I'm staying here until they get me some results. There's a bloke who owes me a favour and he's working on it right now. He's dusted for prints and got nothing. He'll send off DNA swabs, but then that's out of his hands. It will take a while as usual and no chance of rushing that. But he is going to disassemble bits of it and see if he can match the fabric, the stuffing, maybe even the thread. He hasn't said as much but I think we're going to be really lucky if there's anything traceable, but if it's been made of the same stuff then it's probably by the same people. That's something."

"Okay. Stick with him. We must be due some luck soon."

"He did say that he's handled what we could call voodoo dolls before and as far as his research goes, a lot of the modern myths surrounding them have been created by Hollywood and horror writers. He just doesn't think a doll on its own is going to have any impact on someone who isn't involved in the dark arts."

"I have to say I can see where he's coming from," Jordan said. "Doris Beetham wasn't the least put out about the thing. She'd just thrown it in the corner. Julie on the other hand was freaked out about it. That's interesting. We still need to be concerned about the old lady though, after what happened before. Let me know what he finds out."

He scanned the room. Everyone had their heads down. He pulled his book towards him. He would update that as much as he could, though there was nothing to record apart from the protection for Doris. His mobile phone was still in the pocket of the jacket he had draped across the back of his chair, and it took him a moment to find it when the buzzing started. The screen showed a number that wasn't familiar. He answered the call.

"Is that DI Carr?"

"It is, who is this?"

"Sorry, it's me, it's Gil. James and Jack's mum."

"Hi there. Is everything okay?" As he asked the question, his stomach flipped. There was no real reason to assume that the witness was in any danger. Nobody knew she had been talking to them, at least nobody should know unless she had chosen to tell them.

"Everything's fine thanks. It's just that, you said I should call if anything happened."

"Yes."

"Well, I was just down the shops. I could be wrong here. I'm probably wrong but you know, just in case, I thought I'd better say."

He waited for her to get to the point.

"It's just that I thought I saw that bloke. You know the one that was in the car and came over the wall. It was quite a way away, but it was the way he was walking. Do you remember, he had a funny thing with his foot?"

Jordan was already grabbing his jacket and waving at John Grice to attract his attention. "Where is he?"

"Well, he was down the end of the avenue."

"Heading north, south?"

"God, I don't know. Right and left is as far as I understand directions. He turned up the entry on the corner. On the left. It goes through to Copy Lane."

"What was he wearing?"

"Oh, erm. A blue jacket, like an anorak thing and jeans, I think, but I couldn't swear to that, they were dark pants though. He was quite a way away when I saw him. I'm pretty sure it was him. I rung you right off."

"Thanks so much, Gil. We'll come and speak to you if that's okay."

"Yeah, course. I'm going back to mine now."

The chances of a car being nearby were next to nothing. He had to try. Jordan put out an alert. A unit from Netherton and another from Maghull were there as soon as they could be, lights and sirens engaged. Though they circled the area and were joined by another patrol after a few minutes, the bow-legged bloke in the jacket was nowhere to be seen.

John Grice drove Jordan to Old Roan and on the way, they listened on the radio to the desperate search. Jordan shook his head as the urgency died away and it became obvious the quarry was long gone.

"Either he's been picked up or he's gone inside somewhere. We can't reasonably knock on every door in the area. We'll go straight to Gil Lamb's house. At the very least she'll be able to confirm the description of his jacket, maybe a bit more. I'll go to see her, you ask around, find out if anyone else noticed him. Pretty unlikely but we should try."

* * *

"I hope I haven't got you on a wild goose chase," Gil said. "I think it was him though."

"Just tell me everything you can remember," Jordan said.

"I was down the shops. The babies were a bit unsettled, so I took them out for a walk. The pram moving sometimes sends them asleep. On the way back I called in at the bread shop. It was when I came out that I saw him. Walking away, he was. Oh yes, forgot to say he had a bag with him. Like a sports bag. Didn't look very heavy."

Chapter 46

By the time Jordan was back on the main road, John Grice was already visiting the shops asking to look at their security footage. Jordan jogged to the other end of the row of businesses and started to ring doorbells. The Chinese takeaway was closed, and Jordan rang the bell for the flat and jigged up and down on his heels as he waited for them to answer. By the time he had roused them, Grice was walking back along the row of units.

"Not many people about, boss. Nobody remembers a bloke on his own in a blue jacket. Then why would you? I've had a look at the live feed at the bread shop, the newsagent's is monitored remotely, and they said they'd get a copy of the last two hours. I've been on to the council about theirs. Trying to gee them up is like trying to plait fog. The best I could manage was that they'll send a copy of the recording to the office."

"What about the bloke at the end? He's got a good set-up and he was really helpful last time."

Grice shook his head. "No go there, it's closed. The roller shutter is down, and the door is padlocked."

"Oh. Odd time to be closed. There's nothing for the takeaway. They said they only turn it on when they're open. In case there's trouble, they said. I do wonder sometimes if people fully understand the idea of security."

As he spoke Jordan strode away heading for the end of the terrace. Grice had to rush to catch him.

"Have we got the address for where this bloke lives?" Jordan asked.

"We must have. I'll give Kath a call," Grice said.

Jordan gripped the bars of the roller shutter over the front window. Although the blind was strong and well-fitted, it was possible to see through the aluminium slats. He pressed his face up close to the metal. Though the shop was in darkness, he could make out the shape of the counter to the rear and the shelves and display units holding goods. There were flat-screen televisions and computer monitors standing on cabinets around the walls, and there was no doubt in his mind that he could see the glint of light on the shiny cases and the corners and edges of some of them. There was a source of illumination but of course, it could simply be a stand-by light on one of the pieces of equipment or daylight leaking in from somewhere.

"Let's go round the back."

There had been recent rain and the broken surface was puddly and gritty. None of the storage units were open. As the day began to fade, they saw lights flicking on in the flats, faint yellow patches smeared across the wet tarmac. Jordan and Grice walked to the end of the row of shops. There were walls and gates behind the two-storey buildings. A narrow balcony ran along the first floor, outside the doors to the homes. There were a couple of plants in pots beside some of them, but there were also bin bags waiting to be disposed of. There was a bike fastened to the railings with a chain. The electronics shop was in darkness. The windows of the flat above were blank sheets.

"Nobody in, boss," Grice said.

"Looks that way. Damn, he was my best bet for coverage."

"Got his address if you think there's any point. It's not far, and he could come and let us have a look. At the least, that'll give us an accurate description. That's always assuming he walked past here at all."

"We might as well," Jordan said. "There's no point just roaming back and forth along Copy Lane. He'll be long gone by now. Come on, where are we going?"

"He's up in Netherton, off Park Lane. Not far from the golf course. They used to call that Dodge City back in the sixties. It was well rough. They say that you only went there if you belonged. It's better now."

Jordan programmed the address into his phone. It wasn't a long drive.

It was yet another estate of ex-council houses which had been bought up. The one they were looking for was no better and no worse than those around it. Ordinary. They rang the bell and heard the electronic Westminster Chimes deep inside the house. There was a camera mounted above the door and another on the soffit aimed down to the road. They waited. They rang the bell again and Jordan peered through the frosted-glass panel, looking for movement. There was nothing.

"Dead end, boss," John Grice said.

"Seems like it. His car's here though. If that is his."

"What do you want to do?"

"Try the phone number he gave us."

Grice took a moment to examine the details sheet on his tablet and then punched in the number.

He shook his head.

"Try it again," Jordan said. He bent towards the door and hooked the flap on the letter box. He crooked a finger, Grice John closer. "Listen."

They heard the mobile sounding inside.

"Turn it off," Jordan said.

As Grice clicked the call button on his phone, the noise from inside died.

"So, he could be asleep. Could be he's nipped out and forgotten his mobile," he said.

"Really, a geek without his phone, hmm." Jordan shook his head. "There's something off here."

There was a narrow alleyway through to the back garden. It was closed off halfway by a tall wooden gate. There was no lock, just a metal handle. As they passed through Jordan looked up and there was another camera mounted just below the guttering. This one was aimed down at the path.

The garden was a square of lawn with shrubs in a bed at the end. Flags had been laid to make a patio outside the back door and a small set of garden furniture stood to one side. It wasn't exactly pampered but not neglected either. It had the feel of something slowly going to seed.

Jordan tried the handle of the door which led into the kitchen. It was locked. There was a light visible in the hallway beyond, and they could see the window in the front door. There was no sign of movement. Jordan thumped three times with the side of his fist against the wooden panel and followed the thumping with a shout. There was still no sign of life. Grice moved to the side of the building and put his hands up against the window, his face close to the glass.

"There's a cup on the coffee table, the fire's burning. It's a gas one, but it's definitely lit. Can't see anything else." As he spoke there was movement at the corner of his eye. He frowned and turned a little. For a moment there was nothing and then the curtain twitched, a little. He wasn't sure. He waited. Yes, it moved again. "Boss, I think there's someone in here. It's odd."

Jordan looked across at him. Grice indicated the drape inside the window. "I'm sure that just moved, slightly, it was more of a flick than movement from a draft, a waggle."

Jordan turned to scan the garden. He picked up a stone gnome holding a lantern.

"Sorry, mate," he said as he pulled back his arm and aimed the lump of coloured concrete at the window in the door.

The glass shattered and he replaced the garden ornament, gave it a pat on the head and then turned to knock out the shattered shards left in the wood. He pushed his hand through the space to reach inside and unlock the door.

Chapter 47

The house was warm, fairly clean and homely. There were a couple of computer monitors on the dining table connected to a personal computer. There was another in the living room on a folding table pushed into the corner. Cables snaked here and there across the floor but were tidily grouped and coiled. There was a Bluetooth keyboard on the cushion of the settee. Speakers stood in front of books on a shelf in the chimney alcove. The place was given over to electronics, leaving the impression of a home that had belonged to someone older and was now lived in by a younger person who enjoyed his gadgets.

The man Jordan had spoken to in the electronics shop lay beneath the window. One hand stretched towards the hem of the draped curtain, the other arm was thrown up above his head. A small wine table lay on the carpet, the legs broken and the top cracked. There were shards and pieces of ceramic scattered across the floor.

John Grice was kneeling beside the man, his fingers on the side of his neck. "He's got a pulse and he's breathing. I'm not sure what to do. I could put him in the recovery position but if he's got a neck injury that's deffo going to do him no favours. Joe, can you hear me?"

Jordan was speaking to the emergency call paramedic. "They want to know if he's bleeding. I've told them he's unresponsive but breathing."

"Yes, that's about it. Looks as though there is blood soaked into the carpet, but I'd have to move his head to see how much. I don't feel happy doing that. His colour's awful."

"They said not to move him unless he has trouble breathing or he vomits. Ambulance may be about half an hour. They said they'll send someone as soon as they can. We're supposed to stay on the line and let them know if he deteriorates."

"If he deteriorates, he'll be dead, boss. I can't get any reaction from him. I don't know how he managed to move the curtain, but I reckon the effort finished him off. If they don't hurry up, we'll lose him." He turned back to the inert figure. "Don't you bloody die on me, Joe. Don't you bloody dare."

There was a faint moan.

"Keep talking to him, John. It could be he can hear you. Listen, are you okay if I do a quick scan around? I think we need to make sure there's nobody still here." He handed over his mobile phone.

"You go, boss. Me and Joe'll just wait here. That's right, isn't it, Joe? Oh, by the way, mate, my gaffer broke your window. Although actually, it was your garden gnome that did it. I never trusted them things. Come on, Joe, open your eyes for me, pal."

There was no response.

The rooms upstairs appeared undamaged and were tidy. Jordan stepped on the outside of the steps and didn't go into rooms unnecessarily. He peered in from the doorway of the two bedrooms, bathroom and toilet. There was no sign of anyone. He had shoe covers, gloves and hair nets in the car, but there was no point going to fetch them now, the scene was already contaminated.

"You okay, John?" he said as he walked back into the living room.

"Hanging in, I guess. I wish they'd bloody hurry up. I feel useless just sitting here."

Jordan paced around the room. Nothing appeared disturbed apart from the little broken table. The PC screen was dark, and he was tempted to waggle the mouse. If Joe didn't recover, this was going to be a murder scene. He pushed his hands into his pockets.

The furniture was dusty and the little lace doilies on the coffee table were crumpled and in need of washing. "Not much of a housekeeper, are you, Joe?" Jordan said. The desk was covered with a fine film of dust. The keyboard was clean, but some of the keys were worn. A thin cable snaked down beside the cabinet which was alongside. Jordan took a pen from his pocket and poked at the thin wire. It wagged freely, and the plastic connector clinked lightly against the wood.

He leaned closer to the cabinet and could see by disturbance in the dust that something which had stood there recently had now been removed. He turned to the window and tipped his head to one side. "I think I hear the siren, John. They've done well." He strode across the room and knelt beside the other two men. "You're okay, Joe. Help is on the way." He opened the front door and stepped into the road to wait for the ambulance.

Chapter 48

Stella was waiting in Copy Lane. As Jordan drove into the car park, he saw her standing by the window, a mug of coffee in her hand. By the time he arrived in the incident room, she had poured him a drink and was waiting beside his desk.

"What's the latest?" she asked.

"John Grice has gone to the hospital. He's going to give us a ring as soon as the doctors bring him up to date. As far as the paramedics were concerned Joe had 'a nasty bash on the head', I'm quoting. When they moved him there was a fair bit of blood underneath soaked into the carpet. They said he was deeply unconscious. They used the Glasgow Coma Scale. I know about that but don't understand it. I just know that his reading was pretty bad. That's worrying because he had managed to wag the curtain earlier. That feels to me as though he was getting worse. It doesn't look good."

"No point speculating, I guess. We'll know when we know. At least you found him when you did. If you hadn't, then his chances would have been much reduced, surely."

"I think you're right. We need to get forensics round to his place in the morning. I've already left a message for Sergeant Flowers. We need someone in the shop as well."

"The six-million-dollar question has to be whether or not this has anything to do with Julie," Stella said.

"It has to, surely. I've got my fingers crossed that Joe's CCTV in the shop was working. Gil Lamb saw that bloke walking away. I wonder if he'd been into Joe's place. It was all in darkness when we were there, and there was no sign of a break-in. Probably should have taken a closer look."

"You didn't have any reason to think there was a problem though."

"That's a bit moot. I thought it was odd that the shop was closed so early. The bow-legged bloke had been seen in the area. I know that we hadn't any real reason to connect Joe with the murder, but he was a witness even though it was very peripheral. I just have this feeling that I should have been more switched on about joining all the dots."

"I think you're being too hard on yourself. No point fretting about it now, is there?"

"Nope. We work with what we've got. I reckon we might as well call it a day. I'll let you know when I hear anything from John."

"Okay. In early tomorrow, I guess?"

"Yeah. I'll be in before seven. That's unless anything happens between now and then. I need to arrange for a patrol to pass by Gil Lamb's place before I sign off."

"You don't think she's in danger, do you?"

"I certainly hope not. I know we can't put everybody under surveillance. After what's happened up to now, I'm worried about them all – Gil, Doris, even Pat Roach to be honest. I'd feel happier if I knew where Paul Palmer was. There are so many threads to this, and they won't knit together. I wonder if Gil's husband is at home tonight. I don't want to frighten her but it's a worry if she's on her own."

"Tell you what, why don't I just give her a ring, friendly like and see if she's by herself."

"Brilliant. Let me know and then I'll decide what we should do about her."

"Will do."

* * *

Penny was in the dining room when Jordan arrived back in Crosby. Documents covered most of the surface of the table. "Ah, sorry. Let me move this lot," she said.

"No, you're okay, don't worry. Have you eaten?"

"I had a fish finger sandwich earlier. I was making them for Harry and couldn't resist.

"That sounds good, are there any left?"

"Let me do it for you. You look all done in, have you had a bad day?"

"It's not been good and there's more to come. We've got a witness in the hospital and to be honest with you, Pen, I don't know why. I had no reason to suspect he was in danger, but this changes things. I'll need to go over some CCTV coverage later and have someone research him in the morning. There was no need up to now."

"Go and take the weight off your feet and I'll bring your butty through."

When she brought the food into the living room Penny hesitated; it looked as though he was asleep. He had kicked off his shoes and leaned back, his eyes were closed. The smell of the comfort food brought him out of his stupor.

"Brilliant." He reached for the tray and his phone rang.

Penny raised her eyebrows as he snatched up the mobile. The sandwich wasn't something she could keep warm for long, and she couldn't eat another plateful herself. She hovered in the doorway.

As it happened, the call was short. He tossed his phone onto the seat beside him and took the tray.

"Good news?" she asked.

"Not really. The witness I told you about…"

"Yes."

"Unconscious and they don't know when or even if he'll come round. That was John Grice, he's leaving the hospital and arranging for a bobby to take over. It's a rotten job, sitting outside a sick room for hours on end, and we're so short of plods we can ill afford it. It has to be done though." He took a bite of the sandwich, and the phone rang again. The screen showed Stella's name, so he passed the device across to Penny.

"Hiya, Stel, he's got a mouth full of supper at the mo. Can I give him a message?"

"Yeah, that's cool. Tell him Gil is okay. Her hubby is home for a couple of days, and they are going to stay with her in-laws. Just because they are, not because of anything that's happened."

"Okay, I'll tell him."

By the time she moved the tray and rinsed the dishes he was snoring quietly. She didn't want to leave him on the settee. The back injury he'd suffered a while ago would give him gip if he slept there. She shook him gently. "Come on, love, let's get to bed. It'll all look better in the morning."

"I need to do my book and look at some footage."

"No, you really don't. You'll be better doing it after some sleep."

He stared at her for a minute and then let her pull him up from the couch and lead him up to the bedroom.

Chapter 49

It was a foregone conclusion that there would be a call from the DCI's office. At least it came at around nine, after Jordan had the opportunity to assign tasks and call the hospital.

"How's your witness?" DCI Lewis asked.

"Still unconscious, no real change. I've got Kath doing an in-depth search on his background. She hasn't come up with anything of note yet. Seems he's unmarried, lived with his mum before she died, and then he inherited the house. The electronic business looks as though it's doing okay. His bills are all paid, at least, so nothing startling there. He has no criminal record that we've been able to find up to now."

"In that case, you think he's just a witness?"

"Barely that to be honest, sir. He had good CCTV coverage which he shared with us and had seen the blokes in the car a couple of times. But…"

"Yes?"

"Pretty obviously it can't just be that. There's something more, but I can't see it, yet. I think something had been removed from the house at the time of the attack. His computer equipment was still there, but there was just something a bit odd about the set-up. If I had to put money on it, I'd say it could have been a laptop that had been removed. We are looking for Julie's. If it wasn't working, it seems logical that she may have taken it somewhere local to have it looked at. That's something that feels interesting."

"Are you telling me you think he is involved with the murder?"

"Difficult to say, but I am becoming convinced he is more than an innocent bystander."

"This is awkward for me, Jordan. I've got a gold team meeting later today and this is not going to wash well with them. Apart from anything else, this is taking up an excess of man-hours."

"Yes, I understand that. I don't see any other way though. We can't keep people safe unless we're there."

"No, but we can keep them safe by finding this killer. Get me something quickly."

"We're working as hard as we can and following many lines of inquiry."

"I'm not a bloody reporter, Jordan. Don't think you can blind me with sound bites. Okay, you can go."

* * *

The team looked up as he walked back into the office.

"Right, that was grim. Come on, guys, let's have a catch-up and see where we are. Kath, send everyone a copy of what you have about Joe Brady. Then I need to find Paul Palmer, and I want to know where that car was before it was torched. We have two men who've been hanging around the edges of this case, and I reckon they're right there in the middle of it. Why, who and where, and how does it all connect."

"Or not," Stella said.

"How do you mean, Sergeant?"

"We've got the thug coming away from Julie's house and another one waiting in the car. Neither of them was Paul Palmer. Not unless both witnesses are completely wrong."

"Where are you going with this, Sarge?" Grice asked.

"Could it be that the two blokes at the house have no connection to Paul and by default Pat Roach?" Stella said. "If that's the case, maybe he has nothing to do with the murder."

"So, why is he suddenly on the scene when his mum is killed?" Jordan said.

"Yeah. That's a good point, boss. But you did say to keep an open mind."

"I did. Let's go back and have a chat with Julie's mum and Pat Roach. If there is a connection, then we must keep digging and we'll find it. Okay, is everyone clear? We need to sort this, now."

Stella held up her hand. "Just before we finish, and talking of Doris Beetham, the lab is pretty certain that the doll that was left outside her house was made from the same fabric as those at Julie's. They also said they are hand-sewn, and my mate down there said he'd put money on it being the same person who made them both. A very amateur job, he said, not a dressmaker or a tailor or even a crafter. Not a surprise but at least it's more information."

"It is but it makes me even more worried about the old woman. Let's get on."

"Stella, let's get down to Joe's house and then on to his shop. I'm not wanting to hassle the techs, but there is one thing in the living room I want to clarify and I'm keen to see if the CCTV has picked anything up. If Sergeant Flowers is in a good mood, he might let us see."

Chapter 50

It appeared that Sergeant Flowers was in a reasonable mood, because at least he spoke to them. Jordan and Stella were outside the shop which hadn't been taped off, but there were cones discouraging anyone coming too close. There was a uniformed officer at the door.

"No tape?" Jordan said.

"Sergeant Flowers thought it would attract so much attention it would be more trouble than it was worth. The whole row is open to the public and has been busy continuously. I'm to stop anyone entering. I don't think I can let you in, sir. He's taped the back off and there's a shelter and what have you."

"Is he inside?"

"Aye, he is."

Jordan dialled the CSI officer's number on his mobile. He was told in no uncertain terms that his presence in the building was neither welcome nor necessary. There was no sign of forced entry, and nothing seemed to be damaged.

"It was the CCTV feed I was interested in. Is it working?" Jordan asked.

"It was," Flowers said. "It's not now."

"Have you turned it off?"

"No, I haven't bloody turned it off. Why would I do that?"

"Well, you said it was on and now…"

"Yes. It had been recording until the bloke who let himself in, with a key by the back door, turned it off. How do I know that? Because I watched him do it. One minute, lovely clear feed, in comes meladdo and poof."

"Is there a good image of him?" Jordan crossed his fingers as he asked the question.

"That depends what you mean, I suppose. There's a lovely clear image. Will it be any good as identification? No. Not unless you wanted to identify his jeans and trainers, both look bog-standard to me, but you're the detective. This bloke knew where the camera was and made damn sure he didn't show it anything of any use. I'll ask the geeks to send you the relevant bit as soon as I can. Won't help."

"It might. Do you see him walking?"

"A bit."

"Is he bow-legged?"

"Is he what?"

"Is he bow-legged, so that his foot is sort of twisted a bit when he walks?"

"A twisted foot? What the hell is that supposed to mean? Just a minute."

Jordan could hear the sergeant mumbling to himself about silly terminology and bloody stupid questions, but he came back on the line quickly.

"Couldn't stop a pig in a passage, as my granny used to say. Bandy-legged, yes."

"Excellent. Thanks, Sergeant, that is very helpful. Have you been to the house?"

"Can't be in two places at once, can I? No, I sent Janice. She's good and we're in touch. Don't go over there bothering her. She's busy."

"Okay. I did see it yesterday anyway."

"She mentioned the fact that you'd been parading around dropping hairs and leaving footprints."

"Sorry. Can you ask her opinion on the cabinet in the living room? It has a lot of dust on the top and it looks as though something has been moved. There was plenty of security coverage at the house, is there anything on there that'll help?"

"The cameras are the sort that download to a computer, and they've collected the ones that are there. They are headed to digital forensics. You'll have to chase that up with them but give the poor sods a chance."

"If there's anything to find, Janice'll find it. I told you she's good. We'll get back to you. How is the bloke that was clocked anyway?"

"No change last time I spoke to the hospital," Jordan said.

"Okay. Let me know if this turns into a murder scene. We'll be doing the best we can anyway, but it'd be good to know. If he croaks, there'll be more paperwork but on the other hand, I'll get overtime for my lot."

Sergeant Flowers wasn't as hard or uncaring as he tried to appear. He had processed scenes much worse than the one they were attending right now. You couldn't let it get to you. You couldn't do the job if sentiment got in the way, and they all handled it the best way they could.

* * *

Doris Beetham looked brighter than the last time they had visited. The family liaison officer thought that it was simply the constant company and that she was able to begin the process of arranging a funeral for her daughter.

"Nothing dodgy happening?" Jordan asked.

"No. I took her to the registry office, and she's chosen a funeral director. They came to the house. It was sad, but the old woman held up well and I think talking about Julie helped her a bit."

"Are you fixed up with a relief?"

"Yes, we've got someone coming in to stay the night. It's getting a bit tricky. She wants to know why there is so much fuss when Julie's dead and to quote, 'It's all over bar the shouting.' I don't think she holds out much hope of you finding the killer, boss. That's not me speaking, it's just stuff she's been saying."

Jordan made sure that the liaison officer was clear that this wasn't just a babysitting exercise and he had genuine concerns for Doris Beetham's safety. "Don't leave her on her own and if anyone turns up at the door, let me know."

* * *

Pat Roach groaned and rolled her eyes when she opened the door. "Bugger off, will you. I'm busy."

"We won't keep you long," Stella said as she stepped forward and put her foot on the threshold.

"No, not today."

As Pat tried to push the door closed, trapping Stella's foot, they heard the slam of another door.

Chapter 51

Jordan was away before either of the women had time to react. He ran along the narrow concrete path across the front of the house, rounded the corner, and sprinted down the side passage. There was no gate. He could see, as he neared the end of the narrow space, a strip of lawn with flower borders around the edges and a washing line strung between two thin metal posts. He ducked under the damp trousers and underwear, tangling with the laundry on the line and flinging it onto the grass as he passed.

If the fence had been sturdy, Paul Palmer might have had more of a chance of escape, but the dilapidated wooden structure juddered and shook as he scrambled to scale the six feet of old, crumbling wood.

He landed on his back among the roses as Jordan dragged at his legs, and he was on his front, arms cuffed behind him, listening to Jordan reading him his rights before he had time to catch his breath.

Pat Roach thundered across the grass yelling that she was going to report both Jordan and Stella for harassment, brutality, and vandalism. Stella brought up the rear, striding across the space as she dragged out her phone to call for prisoner transport.

"Don't be so bloody stupid," Pat Roach screamed. "He hasn't done anything. You have to be out of your mind. Evading arrest — what arrest? You're scraping the barrel and just looking for anyone to make it seem that you're doing something. This is so wrong and look at my bloody washing."

"If he's done nothing wrong, why did he run?" Stella said.

By now windows had flown open and neighbours were yelling down to Pat asking if she needed help and if they should call the cops. A couple of them inevitably began filming the scene.

Jordan dragged Paul to his feet and propelled him forward towards the house. "I think it's best if we take this inside."

"Well, wipe your bloody feet," Pat Roach shouted.

Stella turned to stare at her in disbelief.

* * *

Paul Palmer was waiting in an interview room. Pat Roach, still complaining at anyone who passed through the reception area, paced and protested until the officer on duty told her he'd write her up for threatening behaviour and a breach of the peace.

Jordan called the hospital where Joe Brady was still in a deep coma. He tasked Stella and John Grice with the questioning and went back to the incident room to catch up on what else had been happening.

There were messages on his phone and after a couple of tries, he managed to connect with Sergeant Flowers.

"I spoke to Janice round at the house in Netherton and she agreed that something had been recently removed from the cabinet beside the computers," Flowers said. "She did suggest that maybe it was the computer the security downloaded to. That makes sense to me and that's how come the bow-legged villain knew where the cameras were in the shop."

"Shit, of course."

"Anyway, while you've been off doing whatever, I've been at this shop. There's a receipt book here, a bit old-fashioned that, especially given the set-up with this bloke, but there's no accounting for what people will do. I had a look at it. If it goes into evidence, it'll be a while before it's seen, so I thought best to have a quick scan now, just in case. This is where my genius and instinct paid off. There is a carbon copy here of a receipt for the repair of a laptop, a Sony Vaio – not surprised it needs fixing, they're out of production by Sony now. Anyway, it was made out to Julie Scott. That's your victim, isn't it? I can't say for sure, but I'll lay money on it that we don't find that particular laptop here. Call it a hunch if you like but it's really skill, knowledge and experience."

Jordan thanked him and went down to observe the interview and passed a note in to Stella that she should ask Paul Palmer what he knew about his mother's laptop.

Chapter 52

Paul was going through the 'no comment' routine. He had refused to have a solicitor, insisting he didn't need one. He had been reassured that it would be provided free of charge but didn't change his mind.

"Where have you been, Paul?" Stella asked. "Last time we saw you was in Blackpool. Pat Roach said you were off on your travels, you'd done with Liverpool and yet here you are, like a bad penny."

"No comment."

"It looks a bit dodgy, you making a run for it like that just now. What were you so afraid of, Paul?"

"No comment."

"Okay. Let's talk about your mam."

He didn't respond but shook his head and closed his eyes.

"Don't want to do that? Okay, what do you know about Joe Brady?"

"Who? I don't know any Brady, what crap are you trying now? What are trying to dump on me this time?"

"Joe Brady. He runs a computer shop near your mam's in Old Roan."

"Why would I know anyone from there? Who was he, her latest screw?"

"Are you saying you don't know him?"

Paul leaned across the table as far as he could. The uniformed officer stationed by the door took a step forward. Stella held up a hand.

"I don't know no Joe Brady. I don't know nothing about my mother's fellas. The thought of her makes me sick."

"Have you got your mum's laptop, Paul?"

He shook his head again and lowered his face into his upturned palms.

"I haven't seen that old bitch. I know nothing about her. I didn't even know she had a laptop. From what I heard she was too stupid and too loopy to know how to use one."

"Yet she had a responsible job, a technical and well-paid position in Liverpool. We know that Ms Roach told you about that. Did you steal her laptop, Paul? Maybe you got your mates to do it for you. Is that where you've been, setting things up to rob poor Joe who was only minding his own business? Did you hope that you could find her will on there? Is that what this has all been about? Did you want to try and fix things so you would inherit what there is of your mother's estate? I bet you thought you were entitled to it. After all, she hadn't given you much in life, had she? Now that the poor woman is dead, it was a bonus for you," Stella said.

"I think Pat Roach told you there was a will and you needed to have a look at it," she continued. "Bit of a worry that, after all, if she died without one, then you'd claim as her next of kin, but a will was a complication. Your chums didn't find one in the house though, so you needed her computer. If she'd left everything to her mam, your granny, well, maybe it was her turn, and she was going to be the next to end up dead. It's so sordid; you do see that, don't you, Paul? They always say, where there's a will there's a relative. She might not have had much, but it was more than you ever managed. Did you kill her so you could inherit, Paul?"

He stared across the table in disbelief. "What the hell are you on? I didn't kill her. I've already told you that. I didn't know she had a will. I didn't even know she owned the house. I know nothing about this. You have got to be joking. This is like something off the telly. I'm not answering any more questions. I want a drink and a sandwich and some paracetamol. You've got my head pounding."

Chapter 53

John Grice, Stella and Jordan sat in the canteen. It was late and the flurry of the day gave way to a more subdued vibe. People still came in and out, food was still sold, but the atmosphere was different.

"What do we reckon, then?" Jordan asked.

Stella put the last few bites of her pastry onto the plate and pushed it away. "I wish I felt more confident. Normally, you know when they're lying. It's in their eyes, in the way they hold themselves, and their little gulps and twitches, especially with suspects who haven't had a lot to do with the police. With him there's been a bit in the past but not enough to make him so cocky. We could do with information from Pat Roach, but she's not talking to anyone now. They've got her in one of the visitor's rooms. She was causing trouble in reception, so they moved her. She won't go home. They had a constable in there with her, but she's tight-lipped and morose apparently."

"Bottom line then. Do you think he killed his mother?" Jordan said.

"I am not convinced. What about you, John, what's your take?"

"I'm with you, Stel. He's annoyed, upset and nervous. He's maybe mixed up in it somewhere, but I just don't get the big guilt coming off him."

"So, where do we go from here? I'm not ready to let him go; have we enough to hold him? Evading arrest won't stick unless we have something more concrete," Jordan said.

"Let me have a bit longer with him. Maybe we can shake something loose. You were right, boss, when you said it was odd that he has turned up now just when Julie gets herself killed. Is that too much of a coincidence? We don't like coincidences, do we?"

"Nope, don't believe in them," Jordan said. "I'll observe."

* * *

"How's your headache, Paul?" Stella placed a plastic cup of Coke on the table. "That might help. It's got caffeine in it."

"I'm okay. They sent the bloody nurse in, didn't they? Blood pressure check and all that shit."

"We have to make sure nothing happens to you, don't we? Don't want our case falling apart because you weren't looked after. It's not the seventies, more's the pity."

Paul picked up the drink and drained half the cup in one go. "What case? You don't have a case. All you've got is imagination. It's just as well me and my mam didn't get on. Just imagine if she'd been any sort of a mother to me. She gets killed and I have all this crap to put up with."

"Ah, but that's the thing, isn't it, Paul? You didn't get on. It must have made you bitter, her giving you up like that. It would me. I just can't imagine how that must feel.

To know that your mother didn't want you. That's horrible, I'd be seriously devoed."

"I was over it, years ago."

As he spoke, Stella was surprised to see him blink rapidly. Maybe there was a raw nerve there, maybe she could poke at it.

"I don't know how you'd do that, do you, DC Grice? I mean, I love my mam. She drives me mad, but she's always been there for me. Reliable, that's what they are, mams."

Grice nodded.

"I met her, she was sound, your mam," Stella said to Paul.

"Not what I've heard," Paul answered.

"Oh right. How's that?"

"Loopy, wasn't she? Oh yeah, she sorted herself out later, but when I was born, she was loopy; a real divvy. That's how come she got rid. So, that's not nice, is it? Later when she got herself together, did she come and find me? She could have done. Didn't even try, as far as I know. Never made any effort. Just washed her hands of me. How nice is that?"

For the first time, there was real emotion fighting for space against the bravado.

"She was scared, you know. Before she was killed, your mum was scared," Stella said.

Paul gave a jerk of his head and lowered his gaze to the tabletop. He began to pick at the skin around his nails.

Stella spoke, quietly. "I know they reckon she'd given up on the spiritualism and what have you, once she got herself together. But that sort of thing sticks somewhere in the back of your mind, I reckon. Anyway, those dolls spooked her."

They waited in silence. Grice realized immediately where Stella was taking this and he shook his head, gave a small tut. "Tell us about the dolls, Paul?"

"What the hell was that for?" Stella said. "Softening her up, were you? A horrible thing to do, torture almost to someone like your mam, someone who was a bit suggestible. Or was it something else?" Stella turned to Grice. "You know what, DC Grice? It seems to me that somebody who would do that might well be a bit mixed up in all that stuff themselves. What do you reckon? A bit woo-woo – into all that black magic and casting spells, devil worship. A real nutter, you know, completely doolally. I mean, it's bloody odd."

"You're right, Sarge. Insane, I'd say. They need locking up going round scaring people."

They waited for him to ask which dolls they were talking about, to tell them he hadn't a clue. For a minute, Paul Palmer didn't speak. He pulled the paper cup towards him and finished the last of the drink. "I'm not."

"Not?" Stella said.

"I'm not into all that crap. All those spells and curses and stuff. But she was, so I thought I'd scare her. I saw them in a film on the telly. The bird in the film was well scared, couldn't sleep and all that and so I thought she deserved it. They were easy to make because they're supposed to look rough. I copied a picture from a website. All that art they made me do in school came in for something."

"But why? Why did you want her to be so scared?"

"Do you have any idea what it's like being in care, being passed from pillar to post? Have you any idea what it's like to lie there scared stiff at night because you don't know if anybody's going to come and drag you out of bed, take you off and make you do stuff you don't want? Do you have any idea what it's like to wish you were anywhere else but where you are because you're so shit-scared that you piss yourself when you hear the doors opening? No, of course, you bloody don't. She didn't either, so I thought I'd give her a taste of it. I didn't know nothing about her except for that. I knew she'd been into it when she was younger. My dad mentioned it, told me how she'd have cards and candles and burning herbs and all sorts of stupid shit. I googled it, you can find out about anything. So, I thought I'd let her know what it was like to be scared. I wanted her to lie in bed at night listening out and imagining. But that's all I did. Yes, I made those stupid dolls, and I left them in her bed. I reckoned she'd have gone running to Pat. Pat would have told me, and I would have faced her then. I didn't think she'd have the police in, did I?

"She should have looked after me, she was my mam. She deserved to be punished for what she did. But I didn't kill her. I was going to face her. When she was scared enough, I was going to confront her and get her to tell me just why she never came to find me. She could have done. She was okay, well off, minted compared to me. She could have come and found me. The trouble was she brought them to you. I never thought she'd do that. The whole thing got out of hand. Then when she was killed, I knew straight away that you'd be able to trace them. I never thought you'd even see them."

"And what about your granny? Why did she get a doll? She wasn't into all of that, and she cared about you. She told us that."

"Yeah, well she didn't do me any favours, did she? I was never going to hurt her or nothing. To be honest I wish I hadn't done that. It was stupid really. It was just that I was frustrated. Julie was dead, and I felt cheated. I had the thing and I thought, why not. It didn't work out the way I wanted."

"Oh, poor you. It didn't work out the way you wanted. I guess it wasn't quite what your mam or your granny wanted either," Stella said.

"No, well, I've already said. That was nothing to do with me. I didn't hurt anyone. I'll hold my hand up to the dolls, okay? But I didn't kill anyone."

Chapter 54

It was raining; a persistent deluge that gurgled in the gutters and flowed in small streams beside kerbs and formed gritty ponds in the potholes. Jordan was sipping at a cup of coffee and staring out into the darkness. He knew what Stella and Grice were going to say when they joined him in the office. He knew that they had requested a change of the arrest warrant for Paul Palmer. He hadn't killed his mother. He had frightened her. But was that all he had done? Now that Julie was dead, there was a real possibility that the CPS wouldn't even think that was worth pursuing.

He couldn't ever say that he understood why Paul had done it. It was a bit pathetic really, but his reasoning had been dark and terrible. An abandoned and abused boy who had wanted his mother to know what he had suffered. How terrible.

It hadn't worked, she had been upset and scared when the dolls were found. She had come home from her holiday to find an intruder in the house. That must have been the worst. Until someone came and killed her. They would never know how scared she had been then. Jordan hoped it had happened so quickly that she hadn't had time for terror. There had been no defence wounds on her hands and arms.

Jordan took a deep breath. They weren't back to square one, but they weren't far off. He went to the desk and replayed the interview video.

As he stomped down the corridor, he met Grice and Stella on their way back to the office. "Where is he?"

"He's in the interview room, boss," Stella said. "I reckon we have to let him go. We can have him for stalking and intimidation, he's admitted to that, but it's not enough to hold him for long. He's going to get bail if we decide to pursue it but..." She shrugged, is there any point now?"

"Where's Pat Roach?"

"They finally got her to go home. Is there a problem, boss?" Stella asked. "Well, apart from the obvious."

"Did he admit to trashing the place?"

"He said he went in," Grice said. "He said he left the dolls in his mother's bed. We didn't ask him specifically. Not once he'd admitted to breaking in."

"But did he?"

"Well. How do you mean; he told us he'd been in there?"

"Did Pat Roach have a key?" Jordan asked. "You know how friends often leave a key with each other in case the cat needs feeding, or someone gets locked out? We all do it. So, did Pat Roach have a key and if so, did Paul Palmer use that to enter Julie's house? If so, is it possible that someone came afterwards. The person Julie chased the night she came back from Majorca, was that Paul Palmer or was it someone else? Someone who had broken in after him and trashed the place and if so, why? You never asked him the date he left the doll, did you?"

"Bloody hell. No, we didn't. We were thinking of the time she found the dolls. After all, that was when she'd chased the intruder," Stella said.

Jordan turned and walked away, turning and speaking over his shoulder. "He could have left them at any time while she was away. He'd know she was away because he was in touch with Pat. I'm going down to have a word with him. I'm going to find out just how he gained access and exactly when, and then we're going back through the whole timeline. I'll be back in the incident room in a few minutes. Brew some more coffee and order some food. I think we might be in for a long night."

As he stormed away, Grice screwed up his face. "I think we might have cocked up there, Stel."

"This thing is so bloody complicated, and it just keeps getting further and further away from us. Poor Julie."

Chapter 55

Jordan came back to the office, tore off his jacket and threw it over the back of his desk chair.

"Right, first off, I don't want you guys beating yourselves up about this. It was an easy assumption. He said he'd been in the house. The house was vandalised – why wouldn't you think he'd done it? However, after speaking to him I don't believe he did. I don't think he knew that it had been trashed. He used a key Pat Roach kept for Julie, as I thought. He left the dolls and that was it. We know that Julie didn't have the chance to tell many people about what was going on with her and in fact, chose not to spread it around. I would have thought she'd have told Pat. If she did, it was never mentioned to Paul, which is beyond strange. Oh yes, he was staying with her while all of this was going on. He moved in when the women went on their holidays. Now he's started talking to us, he's not bothering to hide anything as far as I can see. He says he knew nothing about a will and didn't even know she had anything to leave. Ironically, if we don't find it, he'll be in line to inherit whatever there is by default as next of kin."

For a while there was quiet.

"Sorry, boss." Stella was mortified. Jordan had told them not to beat themselves up about the interview, but it was a disaster as far as she was concerned. She looked at Grice and he couldn't meet her eyes. She straightened her shoulders. It was done, they'd done a crap job and it didn't matter how the boss tried to spin it, she should have done better. She ran the interview video again. Maybe there was something on there to make her feel better. There wasn't really.

They went through some of the notes. Pizza arrived and they left the coffee and pulled three cans of lager out of the fridge in the corner of the incident room.

"It has to be that bloke, doesn't it? The one that Gil Lamb saw climbing over the fence," Grice said.

"I reckon so, and he's the one who has been into the electronics shop. Sergeant Flowers is sending a copy of the video. We are going to get a look at him. Only his lower body by all accounts, but it's more than we had before and oddly in this case it's really useful given his peculiar gait. So, we are much further on than we thought. It's all about Julie's laptop. I don't see any other explanation. I'll admit I can't see why yet. We need Joe Brady to wake up, and soon," Jordan said.

It was after midnight by the time they called it a day and locked away all the notes and books.

Penny was fast asleep when Jordan arrived home. She barely stirred as he slid under the covers. The next thing he was aware of was a weak sun shining through the window, and her standing beside the bed with a cup of coffee in one hand and his mobile phone in the other. "Stella rang, she wants you to call her back."

He hoped that it was news from the hospital. It wasn't, but Stella was buzzing with excitement. They had been able to trace the car's route back from where it was set alight. "Kath did it, boss. She was in before six this morning because she knew she was nearly there. She's been able to pick it up multiple times on the way back to a used car place in Kirkby."

The vehicle had been hidden in plain sight on the forecourt of a down-at-heel showroom until two men had collected it and driven through the suburbs along quiet roads to the industrial estate. "The big thing," Stella said, "is that there is a view of the two blokes. Useable possibly."

"Fantastic. I'm on my way in."

Chapter 56

Kath was buzzing when Jordan arrived at the office. "It's so tedious this viewing," she said. "Hours and hours with not a lot happening and then you get a break and suddenly it's all worthwhile."

The used car lot didn't have coverage of their own, but the small timber yard opposite had a camera that took in the road and frontage.

Kath consulted her notes and then scrolled back through the video on her screen to the point on the timeline where she'd noted the car leaving the lot. "I still have to log the journey from Old Roan to the sales place but that will be fairly straightforward now. The main thing though is the blokes."

They watched as two men crossed the patchy tarmac of the parking area and Kath pointed with her pen at the taller of the two. "Here's Mr Bandy-legs. I wonder what happened to him. Years ago, you would have blamed it on rickets, but surely not now. He must have had an accident or something."

The bow-legged man walked around to the rear of the car, opened the boot and lifted in a jerrycan. Both the driver and passenger spent a couple of moments settling themselves. They turned on the interior light and had an animated conversation with lots of pointing and hand waving. Zooming in several times revealed reasonable images of their faces.

"It's better than we could have hoped for," Jordan said. "We'll get these out on the internet and the television news, the *Echo* website and the hard copy editions of the papers. We need all-port alerts out, and let's get something on HOLMES. Once they know we can identify them they'll be in the wind so, alerts out first, then press coverage and what have you. Brilliant work, Kath."

The atmosphere in the room was upbeat, finally they were making progress. It lasted until mid-morning when the call came from the hospital to tell them that Joe Brady had died without ever regaining consciousness.

Jordan was determined that they mustn't lose the momentum. It was surely the case that the man in the shop, the one Gil had seen walking away, was the one in the car, and he had to be involved in the killing of Julie Scott. Nothing else made sense. The big questions were why, and where the men were now.

By late afternoon, he felt that they had taken enough precautions and that if the suspects made a run for it, they would be picked up at any of the ports or airports. The Channel Tunnel was covered, and forces up and down the country had pictures of the two men. At shift change, all the patrols would be alerted, the net was cast as wide as it could be.

Jordan wasn't going to sit and wait for things to happen. Grice needed a boost to his ego after the debacle of the interview and he sent him off to the car sales unit with a uniformed officer and images of the two men in the car. They didn't expect it to give them much, but it had to be done. It might add to the panic the suspects were feeling if they knew where they'd been seen. There was always the off chance that the showroom owner was innocent of any wrongdoing, but nobody was holding out much hope of that.

* * *

153

Pat Roach sighed loudly when she saw Jordan and Stella standing on the doorstep. "Not you two again. What now?"

Stella pulled the printouts of the images from her folder. "Do you know either of these two, Pat?"

The other woman glanced at the pictures. "Nope."

"Could you look a little more closely? We reckon they might have known your friend Julie." Stella held out the leaflets, but Pat refused to take them.

"I said, didn't I? Don't know them. Now, I've stuff to do."

"Are you not back at work, Pat?" Jordan asked.

"Doesn't look like it, does it?"

They asked if Paul Palmer was still staying with her and for a moment she pursed her lips. It looked as though she wasn't going to respond, and then the young man appeared in the hallway behind her.

"Oh, look, you might as well come in. You're going to get me talked about, standing on my step."

The house was closed up and stuffy, the curtains still partly drawn despite the sunny afternoon. On the table were a couple of empty plates, and the smell of pastry and onion lingered in the air. There were two half-empty beer bottles on coasters.

"Lunch at home, is it?" Stella said. "Been down Greggs, have you?"

Neither Pat nor Paul responded, but Pat picked up one of the bottles and swigged from the neck, wiping at her lips with her thumb and fingers.

Jordan showed Paul the pictures and saw no sign of recognition as he took the leaflets and moved to the window to take a closer look. Now that he had nothing more to hide, he was relaxed and calm. He gave the pictures back. "No, don't know them. Sorry." As he spoke, he sat on the chair opposite where Stella and Jordan were perched on the edge of the settee. "Can I ask a favour, mate?" He spoke directly to Jordan. "I know you've no reason to help me and that. I gave you the runaround, but I've been thinking, and I guess you're the best person to ask."

"I'll help you if I can but if you're going to ask me to interfere with the CPS and the charges against you, forget it."

"No, it's nothing like that. I reckon I'll just wait and see what occurs with that. I did it and I've admitted it. Let's be honest, in the face of everything else that happened sticking a couple of dolls in Julie's house isn't much."

"You might think it's not much," Stella said, "but it terrified your mam."

Paul Palmer looked down at his bare feet. "Yeah, okay. The thing is, though, it's made me consider all of this, everything that's going on, you know, and I was wondering, well hoping, really, that you could ask my nan if she'd meet up with me. I don't want to just go round there. She wouldn't know me from Adam, and I don't want to get into more trouble. What do you think?"

Jordan didn't speak for a while, and when he did, he promised that he would have a word with Doris Beetham if she seemed strong enough. If she was in favour and only if she had no doubts, then he would see what could be arranged.

Paul gave the closest thing to a smile they had ever seen on his face.

"What's going on with you and your work, Pat?" Since her off-hand dismissal of the question, it had niggled at Jordan.

"Finished me, didn't they? I was on a contract from a secretarial agency, and they just said, don't come back. I blame you lot and all this bloody palaver. Even the agency is being a bit leery now. Don't know when they might have something. Not sure if they'll be able to find anything for a while. Cocked things up good and proper, all this."

Stella bit back the comments about Julie and the devastation caused to her mother.

Chapter 57

As they left Pat's house, Jordan gave his car keys to Stella. She pulled the Golf away from the kerb as he booted his tablet computer to read quietly for a while. For the first time since she had started working with him, she felt awkward. The interview with Paul Palmer had been a disaster. Whenever she replayed it mentally, her stomach lurched. She had thought they were acing it. They had him on the ropes and he admitted what he'd done. But they had missed important information. They had both done the interview course and should have known better. John Grice brushed it off and put it down to experience. "We'll learn from it, Stel," he had said when she told him how mortified she was. She could talk to Jordan about it, but what could she say? They had made assumptions and failed to clarify things. Jordan had been nice about it because that's the way he was, but it would be in the records and if there was any reason for an outsider to review the case it would be obvious. He'd rescued the situation, but needing rescuing by the boss hadn't been part of her career plan.

Jordan turned off the minicomputer and shifted slightly in the seat so that he could look more directly at her. She felt her palms begin to sweat. Was this when she got a bollocking?

"I know it might be a long shot, but if we can swing it, I would like to take Saturday afternoon off. Nana Gloria is coming up. Will you come round? She often asks about you. We're going to have the last barbecue of the year, even if it rains, so dress appropriately," he said.

She smiled at him, but she sort of wished he wouldn't be so nice, so fair. It made her feel worse. She blinked rapidly to clear the tears of frustration as they turned into the car park at Copy Lane.

* * *

They were prepared for the reaction to the appeal. DCI Lewis managed to bring in a few more civilian clerks and a couple of volunteer PCs who wanted to make the right impression. The phones were already backed up with calls. The two men, especially the one with the unusual gait, had been seen everywhere. Members of the public who had been at school with friends who broke legs in all manner of bizarre or horrific ways were convinced it must be their mate because he was left with a limp. Fans of Dr Google had researched all the many reasons for the deformity and thought they'd better let the police know what they had found. All the calls had to be recorded and the callers had to be listened to, even the ones accusing the force of ableism. It was always the case, but among it all might be the one fact that would prove vital. The knack was spotting it and that came with experience and sometimes just dumb luck.

Chapter 58

Any calls about sightings that looked as though they had value were passed through to Stella and Grice to be followed up.

There was the possibility that the two men had slipped out of the country before the blocks were in place. There were ways they could be smuggled out even now, given the right contacts and enough money. Everyone knew that, but all they could do for the moment was to keep the faith.

Now that the investigation had become a murder inquiry there was a change in some procedures, but Jordan hung on to it as SIO. It didn't take very much to convince DCI Lewis that there was a connection, but it all added to the pressure.

There was trouble at Old Roan when a few customers tried to collect equipment they had left for repair in the electronics shop near Julie's house. They were told everything was in police hands for the foreseeable future. Just because the electronic devices had belonged to third parties, didn't mean Joe Brady hadn't used them. The laptop belonging to Julie hadn't been found in the workshop at the back of the shop or anywhere in Joe's house. Jordan went back to the address in Netherton. The SOCO team were still there, bagging belongings and turning out drawers and cupboards. There were evidence tents on the gory carpet and, Jordan noticed, the top of the cabinet which had been covered in a layer of house dust was smeared with fingerprint powder.

On the one hand, it was a comparatively simple case. They already knew what had happened to Joe Brady. He had a severe head trauma and he had died from his injuries, no mystery there. They even had a good idea why, they even believed they knew who, but none of that was any help in finding the perpetrators.

DNA swabs had been sent off, hairs and skin flakes collected, films and still images recorded. It had to be done – when the case came to court there must be proof that all the i's had been dotted.

Jordan stepped along the plastic tiles that had been laid down to mark out the safe route although everyone knew he had already left minute traces of his previous visit to the house.

There was nothing for him to do here, just now, and he was aware he would be getting in the way if he hung around, but the visit helped him focus. There was a crime scene manager in place now and he pointed to the rear window when Jordan asked for Sergeant Flowers. "Out in the garden shed. He reckoned you'd be along. Said to tell you that he's busy and if you've nothing to contribute, to leave him alone." Ted Bliss held up his hands, palms outward. "His words not mine."

"It's fine, I understand, but I just needed to revisit the scene."

"You were with the poor bugger before he died, weren't you?"

"I was and I'd spoken to him previously. I thought he was a decent bloke. I reckon he got himself mixed up in something dodgy though. What I need to find out is whether he was aware of it or not. I'll leave you to get on with things. Let me know if anything comes up."

"Of course, but apart from a couple of nosey neighbours, there's been nothing unexpected."

Stella called as he walked back to the car which was parked beyond the rectangle of blue-and-white tape. "You need to check your messages, boss. Something has just come in from the lab, it's a bit of a puzzler."

Chapter 59

Jordan scrolled past the list of messages on his phone until he found the one from the lab. It was from Stella's mate, the one who had disassembled the doll from Julie's house. They had recovered a couple of partial prints from the plastic eyes. They didn't think that they would be enough for proper identification or to use in evidence, but that wasn't really the point. The report was matter of fact, a simple statement of the findings. They were convinced that partials on the broken ornament at Joe Brady's house were from the same person. There were many more items to process, and they were hoping to find full or at least better examples. But this friend of Stella's was switched on and remembered the odd little figure he'd handled and was of the opinion that they were from the same person. The prints were not found on the doll from Doris's house.

Paul Palmer had originally refused to give them prints or DNA. Once he was arrested, he hadn't been given a choice and they weren't surprised to find his prints on the dolls. He had admitted to handling them. Julie's had been there and several others from one individual which were also found in the kitchen. It was this other that had generated the message.

Jordan texted Stella.

> *Tell your mate I owe him. I'll be back at the office in about twenty minutes. Grab John we need to talk.*

* * *

They gathered in a corner of the busy incident room. Around them, the hubbub of call-answering and note-taking continued. Jordan pointed to the report on his tablet.

"It's not Joe Brady, we already have his prints from stuff at his house. There is no reason to suspect he had anything to do with the dolls. The thugs who killed him may well have left their prints unless they wore gloves, of course. If there are any, we can only hope that they'll be on the system. If, as we suspect, at least one of them was in Julie's house, then that wouldn't be a surprise," he said.

"Joe's house is full of prints," Jordan continued. "He wasn't very keen on housework. Some of them could even be from his mum before she died, it'll take ages to log them all. But there is no reason to think they would be on the dolls, not Joe's. Paul's can't be at Joe's. It has to be that whoever was at Joe's had been to Julie's at some stage and had handled the dolls."

"You would though, wouldn't you?" Stella said.

"If you were in there rooting around and you found those weird little things, you would look at them. You might poke at those googly eyes. They were the sort where the pupil inside jiggles."

"So, there's a strong connection between Julie's house and Joe's."

"Have we got Pat Roach's prints?" Stella said.

"I don't think we have," Jordan answered. "You know she's been in this right from the start. She was on holiday with Julie when Paul was sneaking in and leaving dolls and someone else was trashing the house. She was with Paul when he made a run for it, and she's still on the scene now. There was no reason for her to be at the station when we pulled him in, but she wouldn't go home. She's not next of kin. He's not a kid who needs a responsible adult."

"She was Julie's mate. It's not surprising that she wants to know what's happening," Grice said.

"Yes, that's true. But why didn't Julie tell her about the dolls? Why didn't she tell her about the break-in? I mean, you just would. I get why she didn't want to bother her mum, but she didn't tell her best mate. Does that not seem odd?"

"She said it was because it was all so horrible. We found the dolls quickly and it freaked her out. Perhaps she was so upset she didn't want to talk about it," Stella said.

"True. I still think you'd tell your mate. If they were as close as we are supposed to think. That aside, Pat never told Julie that she was in touch with Paul, did she?" Jordan said.

Stella shook her head. "Not as far as we know. Now that does seem odd to me. I mean, why wouldn't you just say something about it? Supposedly she wanted to get them back together. Surely the first step would be to mention that she knew where he was."

"Yes. And here's a thing," Jordan said. "Did Pat know about what Paul was doing with the dolls? Julie didn't tell her but did Paul?"

Stella was about to respond that of course, she did; instead, she stopped and frowned. "We don't know. It's never been confirmed."

"Exactly. If she didn't, why encourage Paul to run away with her? Exactly what was she running from? Having a friend murdered is pretty ghastly but thinking that you'll be next isn't a common reaction unless it's gang-related and we have no sign of that, yet."

"I want Paul Palmer back here tomorrow, just for a chat," Jordan continued. "It feels as though he's on our side at the moment and he does want a favour with regard to his granny. In the meantime, I want Vi to contact the employment agency and find out everything we can about Pat's previous work history and why exactly she has been dropped by the place where she and Julie were working. If we go round there now and ask for her fingerprints, we'll spook her, so let's hold off for the moment. If Paul will play ball with us, we can get them anyway. We just need to make sure it's all above board."

"Okay. I'll sort that, boss."

"The lab will be packing up for tonight so there's not much more we can do with that now. I'm staying for a while to go through more sighting reports. Those blokes are out there somewhere, and we can't miss them."

Grice and Stella glanced at each other. Another Friday night would be spent in the office, reading reports, and making follow-up phone calls.

"Shall I send out for Chinese?" Grice said.

Chapter 60

Many of the civilian staff had gone home. There had been the bustle of shift change in the station and now it was calm. There was the drone of a vacuum cleaner being pushed around somewhere, and now and then voices were raised, sometimes in anger, more often general banter.

They'd eaten the takeaway and had a can of lager each. Now they focused on the reports. Now and again, they'd throw ideas back and forth.

The call from Newcastle came in at just after nine o'clock. A detective about to clock off after a rest day, followed by a day in court, and a celebratory drink after a good result. He had checked reports and notices and seen the requests regarding the two men on the run. The call was directed straight to Jordan's desk. "DS Atkins, sir. I don't know how much help this will be. Your runaway with the deformed legs? I thought someone would have been in touch, but there we are."

"I'm listening, Detective Sergeant."

"About three years ago we had a nasty incident with a couple of minor rogues which involved one of them hitting the other with his SUV. He ran him over and then reversed as he lay on the ground. Obviously, the idea was to finish him off. God knows how he survived, but he did. By the time it came to court, he was mobile, but his left leg was deformed, leaving him looking bandy and his foot at a slightly unusual angle. Apart from that, which was enough to be noticed at a casual glance, he was six-two in height. IC1 with brown hair and hazel eyes. I've sent you his mug shot."

"Excellent, what else can you tell me?"

"I've sent his record. Generally, he's a low-level thug. Nothing major league. Dealing, of course, possession, the odd TWOCING – just nuisance stuff really that gets him into bother. He's been in and out of the nick since he left school. His prints and DNA will be on the database. Doesn't seem to settle anywhere for very long so I can't give you any sort of fixed address. You should have all we've got on him by now, and I'm off for a broon. Enjoy your night."

Jordan turned to the others. "That might have been helpful."

"Excellent, is there something else, boss?" Grice said. "You look a bit puzzled."

"Yeah, what's a broon? He said he was off for a broon."

Grice grinned. "I know that one. It's a bevvy."

Jordan shook his head. "Give me strength, why can't people just speak the Queen's English."

"That'd be the King's," Stella said.

Jordan glared at her. "So, Richard Carl Guthrie. He sounds promising. We have no idea where he might be, but it's more information to get out there."

The next call came from the digital forensic laboratory.

"Jordan? Stevo here."

"Sorry – oh Steve?"

"Yeah, from digital. Listen, I've been following your case. I heard about the dolls and that, weird or what?"

"Yes, very weird. What can I do for you, Steve?"

Jordan finished the call, the other two were looking at him hopefully. "Steve the Geek," he said.

"Oh him. He's well weird, they do say that he sometimes sleeps in the lab just so he doesn't have to waste time travelling to work. That's not right. I mean, I'm in favour of people being keen but there has to be a limit," Stella said. "Anyway, what did he want? It was impossible to follow the call just listening to half of it."

"He's found Julie's will."

For a moment there was silence.

"How the hell can that be?" Grice said. "He's down in the digital forensic lab and they don't have her computer. Oh, unless it was one of those from the shop."

"No, it wasn't, but what they did have was a Kindle. It seems that there's an app you can use to put your own documents, from your PC or laptop, whatever, and make them into a document on Kindle. You can't change it on there and maybe that was the point and it's safely stored away and, you'd have to know it was there to look for it. Steve saw we were looking for documents on her computer and he just went on the hunt with what they'd got. But that's not all. There were other documents on there and, I quote, he thought we'd be stoked when we saw them."

They looked at the clock. It was nearly ten and they were all exhausted.

"You know what," Jordan said, "I reckon we should leave this until tomorrow. Whatever these things are, we need to have a clear head when we see them, and it's not going to make much difference to anything at this stage. I'll go through the information about Guthrie and circulate anything that'll help and make sure it's out on the system. There's a mug shot so that's going to be a boon. But you guys get off home and I'll see you in the morning."

Nobody argued.

Chapter 61

Jordan was struggling to interest Harry in a spoonful of porridge. It was Saturday morning and he wanted to give Penny a bit of a lie-in. He knew he was going to be out a lot, maybe the whole day. She was driving into Lime Street to collect Nana Gloria. Penny and Lizzy were going to organise everything for the barbecue and although he fully intended to be back in time, they both knew that it could be a flying visit, or he wouldn't make it at all. He had spatchcocked and marinaded the chickens and prepared a loin of pork the night before, but that was all he'd managed.

They could have cancelled the whole thing. Nana Gloria would understand, and she would be surrounded by family in London, but he wanted to see her.

The documents from Steve the Geek were open on his laptop and he was trying to get to grips with what he was reading. Between splashes of porridge and sticky fingers, it was a lost cause. He pushed the machine aside to concentrate on his son.

His mobile chimed and Stella's name popped on the screen. "You're on speaker," he told her. "Mind you, it's only Harry here and he's promised not to repeat anything he hears, so go ahead."

"Hiya, Harry. So, have you had a chance to read that stuff from Julie's Kindle? I was up for hours last night deciphering it. The will was straightforward up to a point. Everything is left to her mother, but there is a document with a firm of solicitors in Liverpool. Doesn't say what it is, just that it should be opened after she's dead. She hasn't left enough to need much legal advice, I don't think, so I don't reckon it's a power of attorney or anything. Okay, Doris Beetham might have been out of her depth but I'm sure a mate could have handled that, or the CAB could advise her. Then I saw the other stuff and I began to get a bit more suspicious. There is something well dodgy here. Just have a look at the amounts of money that were being shifted around. I know she was in finance, but from what we have learned all she did was suggest ways for customers to invest their savings or set up pensions. Small stuff in the great play of things. These, on the other hand, are big numbers. I'm not clued up enough to work out where the money is or even whose it is, to be honest, but she's kept those records for some reason and put them somewhere nobody would think to look – unless, of course, the nobody was Stevo. I reckon we need the Financial

Intelligence Unit involved, and I reckon it might explain a hell of a lot. If this stuff was on her computer originally, I'm not surprised it's become the Holy Grail for somebody."

"I need to study this, and we'll have a meeting in an hour. That'll give me time to scrape Harry's porridge out of my hair and for you to contact John."

"I'll see you at Copy Lane, boss. I'll bring bacon butties, a man can't work on porridge alone."

* * *

They printed out the documents because trying to read the rows of figures on screens was difficult. None of them were financial experts and though Jordan had worked with Serious and Organised Crime it soon became clear that they needed outside help. Jordan called DCI Griffiths and gave him a quick rundown on what they'd found so far.

"I reckon we have something here, could be drugs, could be money laundering. Whatever it is there's a lot of money going through the company that both Julie and Pat Roach worked for. I don't know if Julie was involved. My instinct right now is that she was just keeping a record. It was hidden away."

"Might be better if we do that from St Anne Street. From what you've told me," Griffiths said. "Send me everything you've got, including the stuff about your errant suspects."

"I will, but I am holding on to Julie's murder, sir. I met her, I feel that I let her down. I need to find out who killed her."

"We'll meet up and discuss. Are you free this afternoon?"

"Not really. Could do tomorrow."

"Fine. Send me all the information."

After he'd ended the call, Sergeant Castle rang on the internal line to tell them that Paul Palmer was in reception. "Said you asked him to come in, sir."

Jordan glanced at his watch. The barbecue was looking more and more doubtful. There was a message confirming that Nana Gloria was safely in Crosby and had taken over most of the food preparation. Jordan grinned and sighed. He loved his job, but sometimes he just wanted to be at home with his family.

Chapter 62

Paul Palmer was nervous and on edge. When Jordan showed him into the lounge instead of an interview room, his shoulders lost some of the tension and he visibly relaxed. They reassured him that he wasn't under caution, and he could walk out at any time.

"We need your help. I know you didn't get on with your mum and there are good and valid reasons for that. But she was a scared woman, brutally killed, and you can't think that's right for anyone."

Paul had perched on the edge of one of the easy chairs and now he slid back on the seat and stretched out his legs.

"Did you speak to my nan?"

"I'm seeing her tomorrow. Julie's funeral is next week on Tuesday. Do you want to go?" Jordan said.

Paul frowned and stared down at his feet.

"It would be nice for Doris to have someone there," Stella said. "We'll be there, of course, and I expect there'll be neighbours, but it would be pretty nice for your nan to have family there. If she agrees, of course."

"Okay, if she wants. I suppose it'd be good. So, is that all you wanted? You could have just given me a bell."

"No, there is something else. We needed a word about Pat."

"Oh aye, what about her?"

"How well do you know her?"

"Yeah, I know her. I knew her when I was a kid, she was with my dad for a bit and then we kept in touch."

"But now, how well do you know her now?"

"Well, I suppose not as much. She got in touch a bit out of the blue, but she said she'd found out where my mam was working, and she'd made friends with her and blah blah and did I want to meet up." He paused and frowned again.

He told them he hadn't been interested at first, and she had continued to call him. When the Spanish holiday had been arranged, she had suggested he come from where he was living in a bedsit in Wallasey and stay in her house. The timing was right. His lease was about to run out and money was very tight. He couldn't see a downside until she suggested that once she was back from Spain, they would arrange the meeting. He felt pressured.

He had taken advantage of the rent-free room, but the more he considered meeting his mother the more he disliked the plan.

"I didn't want to do it. I just got more and more angry about everything that had happened and then I came up with the idea about the dolls. Because I was so near, and I knew she was away. It was stupid, really bloody off the wall. I was on my own and going over and over stuff and I was just a total nutjob, I mean I see that now, and it was pointless as it turned out. But I couldn't have any idea she was going to end up dead. That was nothing to do with me."

Jordan took out the image of Richard Guthrie. "Did you ever see this bloke around?"

Paul took hold of the printout. "I don't think so. He looks a bit familiar, but I was in care, loads of lads came and went. Who is he?"

"We think he might be involved in Julie's murder, and we are pretty sure he killed the man that owned the electronics shop."

"Oh aye, I saw there'd been trouble there. I didn't know him. I know you asked me about Joe Brady, but I didn't know who it was. I went in once, but that's all."

Jordan felt the buzz in his gut, the one that told him when a casual comment was far from incidental. His face remained passive. "Why was that?"

"Pat asked me to go in. She had a laptop with him, and she asked me to collect it while she was on holiday. But I never got it. She wasn't there, so she didn't need it and I reckoned she was just giving me something to do. Anyway, I couldn't get it, so I didn't hang around. I did go in, but the bloke was busy with some stupid woman trying to buy a telly. I was going to go back later."

"How were you supposed to collect it?"

"What do you mean?"

"He didn't know who you were. Did you expect him just to hand over a laptop because you said so?"

"Oh, I see. No, she had the receipt. But as I say I never used it."

"What happened to the receipt?"

"I told her I'd lost the bloody thing. She gave me down the banks about that. Anyway, it was gone, and she was livid."

"Have a search for it, will you. It might be really helpful if we can see that," Jordan said.

"It's gone, mate. I didn't tell her, but I left it in my jeans, and it went through the washing machine."

Chapter 63

"Did you not look at it, Paul?" Stella asked.

"Not so much. Pat told me what it was, and then it was mush."

"The one we're looking for would have your mam's name on."

"Would it?"

"That gives us a problem," Jordan said. "Especially as you seem to have 'destroyed it'."

"How's that?" Paul shifted, pushing himself more upright. He detected the change in the atmosphere.

"You already told us you'd been in your mam's house while she was away."

"So?"

As he caught the implication of what Stella had just said he leaned towards them, tense again.

"Hey, hang on. You'd better not be suggesting I nicked it. Why would I? What would I want with some clapped-out old laptop. I've got my own."

"Maybe for what was on it," Jordan said.

"Why would I want what was on it? What was on it? No, don't tell me, I don't want to know. I didn't even know it was hers, did I? How would I know that? Even if I knew she had one, I couldn't have known it was in the shop. This is last, this is. I'm being set up. That's it. I'm gone." He stood and leaned forward, leering at Jordan. "You had me there, mate. I believed you for a minute, thought we had an understanding."

Before either of the detectives could speak, he stormed from the room. They heard his feet pounding down the corridor and then demands that the front door be opened to let him out.

"I think he's gone," Stella said.

"You could be right. Was that overreaction?"

"It was a reaction, certainly. I suppose it's fair to say that he was on edge all the time and just waiting for an excuse to leave. He didn't need to tell us about the receipt, did he?"

"No. I don't think he saw anything dodgy about it. Interesting that Pat wanted it collected while she was away. Maybe she didn't want the electronics bloke to recognise her and know she wasn't the one who took the computer in. I think she nicked the receipt from Julie. There was no reason for Julie to give it to her. So, why? We might not have got quite what we wanted but I reckon this was worthwhile," Stella said.

"I don't think we have enough to pull her in yet. We only have Paul's word that she gave it to him, and he hasn't exactly covered himself in glory up to now."

Jordan glanced at his watch. It was after two. There was very little more for them to do. There was the meeting with DCI Griffiths on Sunday morning and things would likely change significantly after that. Much of the investigation into whatever it was that Julie had hidden on her Kindle would be diverted. Jordan had accepted that, but was determined the murder was his to solve.

"Back tomorrow and we'll review what we have. I don't think Paul killed Julie. If he had, would he want to meet his nan; would he have come back to Liverpool? There's no need. I think he is still drawn to Merseyside as home and doesn't feel the need to run. It was Pat that said he'd gone. That leaves us Mr Bandy-legs and his mate or A N Other. We need to find them," he said.

"We've done all we can for now, boss. Kath and Vi are researching what we have of Guthrie's background. Nothing new has come up. His family is gone, scattered and lost, and he's never held down a job – not even a dodgy one that we can trace."

"I think we could do well to go back to the car showroom. I know the owner was questioned and denied any knowledge but let's give him another looking at. I'll have a word and see if we can bring him in. Might put him off balance having him away from his home ground. I'll try and set that up tomorrow. No point calling the DCI now, he won't appreciate being called on the golf course. In the meantime, there's some of Nana Gloria's spicy rice and a lovely bit of pork round my place that should be well on the way to being perfectly cooked. I'll see you there."

Stella hesitated for a moment, she could go home and review files. She could do her laundry and some more cleaning up in the flat that was looking good now the work was finished. Then again, she had tasted Jordan's barbecued pork before.

"See you in Crosby, boss."

Chapter 64

When the patrol car arrived at Boyle's Cars in Kirkby, Alexander Boyle, Sandy to his mates, assumed it was a routine call to have a quick look around his premises and check the vehicles. "Can't you come back tomorrow, lads? I've just made a cuppa and I haven't had a bifter yet. I need my fag and a coffee. If you want to wander about on your own, help yourself. Otherwise, give a bloke a break. Tell you what, you do me a solid now and when the missus is looking for a new runaround, we'll have a chat. There's nothing here for you anyway."

They asked him to accompany them to Copy Lane and watched in cynical amusement as he 'threw a genuine wobbler'. He huffed and blew and argued but when they told him they couldn't leave without him, even if that meant they had to hang around all day, and what that would do to his weekend trade, he gave in and locked up the shabby office. He refused to travel in the marked car and followed behind in a blue Mercedes, shiny and almost new. Much better than the clunkers that were offered on his forecourt.

Jordan kept him waiting as long as he could given that he had a meeting with DCI Griffiths in the early afternoon. By the time he entered the interview room, Sandy was beyond livid. Jordan sat quietly while the car salesman ranted and fumed. He told him he could have left at any time and that he wasn't under arrest. This made him rant even more as Jordan had assumed it would.

"Mr Boyle, we have a couple of very quick questions and then we'll leave you in peace. Always providing we like your answers, of course."

He laid a picture of Julie Scott on the table between them. It was from her personnel file and showed a smart, smiling woman. Then he overlaid it with one of the crime scene pictures. Sandy Boyle gasped and turned away, covering his eyes with his hands.

"Jesus, mate. That's last that is. You shouldn't be showing people that."

"I'm not," Jordan said. "I'm showing you. I want you to know just what we're dealing with here. This woman had just come back from her holiday to find some scroat had broken into her house. She told us about it but before we could find out who it was, this happened." He picked up the image and held it in front of Boyle's face. "I want the bloke who did this."

"Well, it wasn't me, was it?"

"I hope not. If it was then I will bring down the whole weight of the law on your head. You'll be in jail quicker than you can blink and forget bail and forget parole. I'll make sure you stay there as long as possible. You'll be an old, old man. No business, no home, nothing. But being upfront, I don't think it was you, otherwise you wouldn't be sitting here nice and comfy with a drink of water and a biscuit."

"So, what is all this? What makes you think I had anything to do with it? Jesus, I might sail a bit close to the wind with some of the MOT failures, nothing dangerous mind. They're a bit overzealous sometimes with the emissions and what have you. I tickle 'em up a bit. Given the way people are struggling now I do them a favour, take the cars off their hands. I give 'em a fair price and everyone's happy. But that..." He pointed at the table. "That's nothing to do with me, never. I donate to the Dogs Trust, me."

Jordan took out the copy of the still from the CCTV at the timber yard. "That's your place. I know it is. That car was parked there, and these thugs came to collect it."

Jordan leaned back in his chair and stretched out his legs in front of him. "Okay, I'm waiting. Who, why, and where are they now?"

Boyle stared into the middle distance. He picked at the cuticle of his thumbnail until it bled. He shook his head. It was obvious to Jordan and the uniformed constable by the door that he was having an internal debate and he wasn't enjoying it one little bit.

"Just a favour, that's all," he said.

"A favour?"

"I can't tell you anything. Yeah, that one" – he pointed at the picture, the driver – "he's a mate of my brother. Said he wanted to put this car away for a bit. That's all I know. I just let them use my place. I didn't ask no questions. Look, it looks a bit dodgy, could have been stolen, could have been uninsured, I don't know. I just did 'em a favour. I know nothing about those blokes. I think I need a solicitor."

"Why?"

"Well, I just don't want to answer any more questions and you can't ask me any now, can you?"

Jordan stomped back to the incident room. Life has become so much harder with all the police procedural films on the television. "John, keep him hanging for a bit and then let him go. We haven't got enough to hold him, and I think he's a bit dodgy but that's about it. We haven't got the time or resources to spend on him right now. Let traffic know about his MOT failures though, we might as well have him for that."

Chapter 65

The offices on St Anne Street hadn't changed since Jordan left, but then it hadn't been long. As he passed by on his way to DCI Griffith's office he noticed that his old desk was littered with files, a couple of cardboard boxes, and a gathering of empty takeaway cups. So, his spot was sort of still there if he wanted it. Somebody had nicked his chair though.

He didn't want it.

Griffiths gave him coffee and there was cake. Jordan couldn't resist and slid one of the slices onto a plate. "Canteen's improved since I was here," he said.

"Ha, I wish. No, these are from a new coffee shop, the Paper Cup, down in Queen Square. It's a nonprofit that offers training to people in need, and I have to say their stuff is great. They do good coffee as well. If this hadn't sounded so heavy-duty, I would have suggested us meeting there. Maybe next time."

"I'll look forward to it." Jordan opened his briefcase and pulled out the files. He had spent the journey into town getting his thoughts in order and now he delivered a rundown on everything that had happened and what his conclusions were.

"So, you haven't made any further inquiries at this Julie Scott's offices?" Griffiths asked.

"Not since the preliminaries. Once I saw the way that this was going, I knew it was probably something I would need to hand over."

"Hmm, it might have been better to have given us a heads-up sooner," Griffiths said.

"I was working through it and my main concern was Julie and what had happened to her. It wasn't clear at first what the motive was. On top of everything else we were thrown by all that crap with the dolls. Once that became clear, our focus changed. Now I believe the main thing from your point of view is Harding and Harding, in the city. I reckon, from what we've seen in Julie's data, is that it's money laundering. We know that could lead to anything and anywhere. Drugs, people trafficking, even just financial fraud." Jordan paused and took a drink.

"It needs forensic accountants to go through what we have and then I reckon that will lead them to the financial advisors. I don't know how big it might get after that and anyway that's more your bag than mine. But, Dave" – Jordan leaned forward and looked the DCI in the eye – "I want to find the people who killed Julie. It's one of the reasons I haven't gone in too heavy at Harding and Harding. I didn't want to alert them to the fact that they'd been rumbled, not yet."

"And these blokes with the car, and the laptop? What's your take on that?"

"I'm still working through that; it's my main focus at the moment. Poor Joe Brady hadn't a clue what he was mixed up in, I don't think. He took in the laptop in good faith. We still haven't found it and we don't know what was wrong with it. It could be Julie cleaned it out anyway. The Kindle record is all we have right now. I don't know what she was intending to do with the data. It could have been she was planning something dodgy herself, maybe blackmail. Of course, she could have been going down a completely different route and intending to blow the whistle on what was going on. Maybe we'll never know for sure. Somehow someone found out what she had. If only she had told us about it earlier, we might have been able to save her. That grinds at me, it really does. Why not trust us when she had the break-in. That could have made all the difference. Maybe she was as confused by the stuff with the dolls as much as we were."

"And Pat Roach?"

Jordan shook his head. "Not sure. She worked with Julie. She knew a lot about her. We've spoken to the agency she was employed through, and they had her on their books for a while. She did bits and pieces of office work for them for a few years and then settled at Harding and Harding. Interestingly, none of the places she had been before wanted her back or wanted her on a permanent contract. They never complained about her but just didn't seem impressed. Maybe we need to speak to some of them and find out why."

"And Julie's murder, is she involved in that?"

"I am trying to decide. I can't see that Pat Roach was wrapped up in money laundering. She had no real responsibility. She was a secretary and not even to one specific person. Just general typing and filing. She has no background in finance. I don't think Julie was confronting her about that, it just doesn't gel. Then again, she was Julie's friend – maybe they'd talked. I need to find out. I haven't finished with her yet."

Chapter 66

Jordan drove back through the Sunday afternoon quiet. The city was never empty, but most of the summer tourists had gone now and there was a game on the television that kept the football crowd off the streets. There were a few cars with red scarves flying out of the windows, and he thought of Terry Denn, his old sidekick, who would no doubt be glued to the screen if he hadn't managed to get tickets for Anfield. He really should arrange a catch-up with Terry, see how he was getting on since his promotion.

He glanced at the clock. There were a few precious hours he could spend now with Harry, Penny and Nana Gloria before she headed to London in the morning. DCI Griffiths didn't have that luxury, and as Jordan left, he had already been lost in the files and online data. He would ring later or, if Jordan was lucky, in the morning with his thoughts. For now, unless Richard Guthrie and his mate were spotted, there was a chance of family time. He'd make a roast beef dinner – Yorkshire puddings and all the trimmings – and open one of the good bottles of wine. He smiled.

The afternoon and evening were a rare treat and the next morning, when Jordan took his nan a cup of hot water to start her day, he had the chance to perch on the side of her bed and spend a last few minutes with her. She told him again that she loved him and was proud of him. She also told him he needed his hair cutting and there was a stain on his shirt collar.

Stella was already in the office when he arrived, and John Grice pulled into the car park behind him. "A quick catch-up in five minutes," Jordan said.

"I'm waiting to hear from St Anne Street. I think that'll ease the pressure a bit. They'll take on the money laundering side of things. The other cases we've got on are ticking over nicely. So, we're going to find those thugs who killed Joe Brady and that will give us Julie's killers, I'm convinced of it. I've already gone through the PNC reports, and there was nothing new. They could have slipped out of the country, but we are going to find them even if they have. I know it's all more complicated now we're not part of the EU, but that doesn't mean we give up."

He left Grice ringing round to other forces reminding them that this was still a hot case. He contacted the press office to arrange more posts on websites and in the papers, and they arranged a briefing for later in the day with DCI

Lewis front and centre with images of the men on the screens behind him. Jordan promised to be there if he could. It was low on his list of priorities.

He collected Stella, and they went to see Doris Beetham.

Although she was still frail, and her eyes and nose were red, witness the regular bouts of crying that accompanied her grief, she did seem stronger. She was dressed in black even down to the handkerchief tucked up the sleeve of her cardigan. The curtains were closed and on the mantel above the gas fire stood a line of cards emblazoned with doves or lilies or crosses floating in unlikely clouds. The sadness was overwhelming.

"They're bringing her past tomorrow," she said, referring to the funeral cortège. "I couldn't have her in here, not with my narrow hallway. It's not her home anyway, so what would be the point? We'll take her to Anfield. My mam and dad are there and Julie's aunty. I'm having her cremated though. There'll be no one to look after a grave once I'm gone and I couldn't bear the thought of weeds. There'll be a drink back here after. I can't do much, but her next door has said she'll go to M&S and get snacks."

Jordan had no response and busied himself straightening a cushion and draping his coat on the arm of the settee.

He expressed his condolences again and confirmed that there would be a police presence at the funeral. "We will be in uniform unless that will upset you, Doris."

"It's nice of you, lad. It'll look nice that, smart. I'm glad."

It was time to tell her about Paul Palmer. Stella leaned closer and placed her palm on top of the crepey skin of Doris's hand. She told her quietly and simply that her grandson was nearby and that he would like to come if she would allow it.

They expected an emotional reaction and sure enough there were floods of tears and questions gasped in sobs, but it was as if they had given her a gift. By the time they left, they knew that Paul would be welcomed and maybe he and his granny could find a way to make some sort of future together.

"Nice to think she won't be on her own," Stella said. "Over to Pat's then?"

"Yeah. We'll let him know," Jordan said. "I think it's going to help the old woman."

"He wasn't best pleased when we saw him last, mind you."

"No but this was his request. He'd better not let her down now."

They pulled up in front of Pat's house. The curtains were closed, the small metal gate at the end of the path left open. The wheelie bin had been emptied but not yet taken back to its place in the back garden, although most of the others in the street had gone.

"Looks as though they're still in bed," Stella said.

Chapter 67

They could hear the doorbell chiming inside. Jordan leaned close to the front door to peer through the fancy-coloured pane. There was no shadow, no movement. The kitchen door at the end of the hall was open and letting in daylight from the back of the house, but no silhouette moved behind it.

He pressed the bell again and rattled the cover on the letter box. Stella walked across the garden and round into the side passage.

Jordan was about to join her in the back when there was the thump of footsteps from inside. A shadow wavered behind the ornate glass. The door opened partway. Paul Palmer stood in the narrow space dressed in a pair of blue shorts and a T-shirt. His hair was dishevelled, and he rubbed at his eyes with the heel of his hand. "What the hell, la?"

"Having a lie-in, are you?" Jordan asked.

"Why, what time is it?"

"It's well after ten. Did you have a heavy night?"

"Nah. I just didn't wake up. Where's Pat? She usually gets up first. I hear her clattering about in the kitchen. She puts the toast on."

"She not here then?"

"I dunno. Come in, I'm bloody freezing my nuts off here. Come in and wait on while I get my trackies."

Stella joined Jordan in the hall. They listened to Paul thumping about above them. The toilet flushed, and moments later he thudded back down the stairs.

"She's not up there," he said. He raised his voice. "Pat, where are you?"

There was no response.

Jordan pushed past and strode into the kitchen. He laid a hand on the kettle. It was cold. There were no dishes in the sink and no sign of anyone having had breakfast.

"Was she going out, did she say?" he asked.

"No. We watched telly for a bit after I got back from the alehouse then I went up to bed, and she stayed. I heard her tidying round. She always washes the dishes before she goes up. Can't stand a mess of a morning."

"Have you looked in her bedroom?" Stella asked.

Paul shook his head. "I don't do that, usually."

"I'll go up, shall I?" As she spoke, Jordan pulled a pair of nitrile gloves from his pocket.

Stella raised her eyebrows and gave a small nod. She dragged a pair from her own jacket.

"Let's just go into the living room shall we, mate?" Jordan said leading Paul out of the hallway.

"What's going on?"

"Probably nothing. We came round to talk to you about Julie's funeral tomorrow. It seems a bit odd that Pat's not here. She's probably just nipped out to the shops though, eh?"

"Not without her cuppa, I don't think. We've got milk, I brought a bottle back yesterday affie. We've got bread and anyway she normally has a drink and a ciggie first."

"Where does she hang her coat?" Jordan said.

"On the hook in the hall." Paul turned and leaned round the door. "Oh, that's odd. Coat's gone, but her bag for life's still there. So, I don't reckon she's gone the shops. She's gone somewhere though. Her shoes and handbag aren't there either."

They heard Stella running back down the stairs. "Her bed's not made, but there's no sign of anything untoward."

"You're wrong there," Paul said. "She always makes her bed as soon as she gets out of it. She rags me about it because I don't bother with mine. She's got this pile of pillows and cushions and a fluffy dog. If she's gone out and her bed's not made, then there is something – what did you call it? – untoward, if that means bloody odd."

Chapter 68

They questioned Paul Palmer to discover more about Pat Roach's habits. They explored his worries that she was acting out of character. Yet he was more concerned with tea and toast and shrugged off the earlier comments.

"Who really knows with her? She's not exactly stable. She's not working at the mo, and she's always been a bit flaky. She used to go off when she was living with my dad, way back. Just up and disappear for days at a time and then back with no explanation. It was one of the things that had them splitting up. He was on the rigs, and she was supposed to be in charge of me. He came back more than once to find that I'd been looking after myself even when I was a little nipper. She's never been what you can call reliable. So, she's gone off. I'm old enough to look out for myself now and I'm comfy here and I reckoned she owed me. Doesn't bother me where she is unless she doesn't pay the rent, then I'm going to be out on the street again. Look, she'll be back, just like a bad penny. Just wait."

He tried her mobile number a couple of times, but it went straight to voicemail.

They told him about his granny and how she had been so emotional. Jordan worried now that, if Paul found himself homeless, he would take advantage of the old woman. There was of course the house Julie had lived in, and they didn't think Paul had thought through the fact that it would more than likely be his. He would be able to move away from Pat and have a roof over his head with only running costs to take care of. His mother had let him down in his childhood, but now, though it was unintentional, she had given him security. It wasn't Jordan's place to mention it and it wasn't the time.

Pat Roach couldn't really be considered vulnerable. As far as they knew she had no health issues, and she hadn't seemed depressed. She was upset about her friend, but that was to be expected. On the other hand, she could be considered a person of interest in everything that had happened. Some of her behaviour had been questionable. Her reasons for running off with Paul were still something that hadn't been fully explained. What had happened now wasn't going to go down well back at Copy Lane when he had to tell DCI Lewis and the gold team that the whereabouts of one of the principles in the whole drama was unknown.

"What do you want to do, boss?" Stella asked, back in the car.

"I don't want to add this to the alert, not yet," Jordan replied. "It could be that she's just gone off for a day in town. She's been under stress. Her mate is dead. She might have gone to buy something suitable to wear to a funeral. She's a grown woman and we don't have any solid reason to assume that she's in danger. I'm not happy though. Not happy with this at all."

They would risk waiting. Paul had agreed to let them know if she came back and anyway Jordan planned to call again at the house before the end of the day. If she hadn't turned up by then, things might have to change. He really didn't want to face Lewis with that.

As they drove back to Copy Lane, the call came in from St Anne Street and it was as they had thought, as they had hoped. There was something very nefarious happening behind the rather ornate doors of Harding and Harding in the centre of the city. DCI Griffiths was assembling a team. What they had was already with the forensic accountants and once the evidence was assembled, the odds were that some people at the firm of financial advisors were in for a very unpleasant surprise in the next few days.

"Honestly, Jordan," Griffiths had said, "you're not even working here now and you're still bringing me stuff like this. You should come back to us."

"No, I'm good here, thanks," Jordan told him. "But don't forget, I want those two thugs. Give me time to find them."

"I can give you a couple of days but that's about it. Once the shit hits the fan with this, I can't make any promises. If we do end up bringing them in, you'll be involved of course."

"Not good enough, sorry, sir, but I have to find them, and I have to bring them in here."

"Well, in that case, you'd better get your finger out, mate."

Chapter 69

Jordan called the agency that employed Pat Roach. They hadn't heard from her and told him, confidentially, that they had taken her off their books. "She was never popular in the places we sent her," the agent told him. "This last time it seems she just didn't go back after her holiday. I mean, I know her friend was killed but that's no reason to let people down."

"Why wasn't she popular at the other places?" Jordan asked.

"She just didn't get on with other staff members. It's not easy doing temping. You have to land somewhere and hit the ground running and a lot of offices are very cliquey. The best temps make a real effort to be helpful and friendly but not too pushy. Apparently, she didn't. I shouldn't say this, but we did ask around. We get to know our clients very well and a few of them said she was seen as a bit of a creep. At her level, sorry but this is true, you should just keep your head down and do the work and not get too involved. If they take you on permanently, that's when you can make your presence felt in order to get on. When it comes to it, the staff do have some say in who is kept on for longer or asked to cover again and she just wasn't liked."

They promised to let him know if she contacted them.

"It's odd," he said to Stella. "Generally, she was unpopular and yet Julie went off on holiday with her. Julie was efficient and pleasant, she'd been at the company for a while, was well thought of and this newcomer, who a lot of people didn't like, became a close enough friend to go away with."

"Yes, but there was the link, wasn't there? The connection with the ex-husband."

"Wouldn't you have thought that would make it less likely that they would get on?"

"Yes, I see your point. People are odd though, aren't they? Who knows what it was? Something to make them close, maybe even moaning about him together, and there was the son. Julie seemed to have washed her hands of him, but can a mother ever do that completely?"

"I suppose there is that. But maybe something else?" Jordan said.

"What?"

Jordan pulled a notepad towards him and began to doodle, writing down names and linking them together. Phones were ringing and there was the bustle of the station at full swing, but he was turned in on himself, his head tipped to one side, his eyes on the paper.

"Listen," he said at last. "We know that Julie had found out what was going on at Harding and Harding. We don't know the details yet, how long and how much or even why. We're not sure what she was planning on doing about it. Whistleblower, blackmailer, maybe just intending to confront whoever was involved and have them do the right thing. That's a heavy load to carry on your own. What if she simply needed someone to share it with? She couldn't trust the full-time staff and yet she had this common link with Pat, much more than with any other temporary help. She had the chance to get away to Spain, maybe she unburdened herself. Sunshine, boozy nights, and away from the stress."

"I can see how that would happen. It doesn't work though, not if Pat had already stolen the receipt for the laptop. She must have known what was on it before they went to Spain."

Jordan frowned at her. "Okay, but maybe that was why they went. Maybe Julie needed to get away before she blew the whistle and she just saw this as a chance. Depending on how high up the rot goes, and that remains to be seen, she could be looking at losing her job. They could talk, decide what was best away from the usual setting. Maybe Julie thought Pat would help her. I do wonder what was wrong with the laptop. Could it be that Julie put it in the shop for safety? She was going away and the house would be empty. As it turned out, she was right. There was a break-in but why then?"

He thought for a little while longer, doodling on the page in front of him.

Unexpectedly, he pushed back from the desk, his chair colliding with the waste bin and sending it spinning across the floor. He grabbed his jacket. "We need Pat Roach's mobile phone records. I'm going to DCI Lewis and have him rush through a warrant. Will you get Kath on that, Stella? You can show up for the press briefing. Don't mention that Pat is missing. Get as many of the team as we can checking shop cameras, door cams, and whatever from around Pat's house. We need to find out where she's gone and who with. Railways! Don't forget the railways and the buses, Arriva, Stagecoach, Merseytravel, whatever there are in the area. Let's do it now."

He left Stella staring at a slowly closing door and the litter of napkins and empty takeaway coffee cups.

Chapter 70

Paul Palmer was still not dressed when he opened the door to Jordan's heavy knocking. "What now? Have you nothing better to do than hassle me?"

Jordan pushed his way into the house which now smelled of bacon and cigarettes. "When did Pat give you the receipt?"

"The receipt?"

"Jesus." Jordan ran his hand through his hair and took a breath. "The receipt for the laptop."

"She didn't, not really. She rang from Spain. I thought it was a bit odd fussing about that when she was supposed to be on holiday, but she said it was important."

"So how did you get it?"

"It was in her coat pocket, her ordinary coat. Look, mate, why are you mithering on about this now? Surely you can get the thing. Police don't need no receipt. Anyway, didn't you say it was Julie's? I don't understand why Pat'd have it at all? But it's gone, I told you I put it in the wash, and it came out in bits. I told her I'd lost it, and she was dead miffed. I told her the bloke in the shop said he'd accept the till receipt instead, though, if I had that."

"So, where was that?"

"I haven't got a clue, la. She did a bit of cursing and fuming and told me what a useless wazzock I was and hung up."

"And to go back to the original question... when was this?"

"It was just before they came back. That's why it seemed so stupid, a couple of days and she could have sorted it herself. She never mentioned it once she got back so I don't know what all the fuss had been about. Hey listen, mate. What should I wear tomorrow?"

Jordan was taken aback by the sudden change in direction. He looked at the young man in front of him, his hair was tangled, his clothes were stained, and he looked lost and unhappy. He'd never really had a chance. There was no Nana Gloria to tell him to smarten up and no mum to make sure he stayed on the straight and narrow.

"I don't reckon it'll matter much, Paul. Just look clean and wear something sober, you know, dark-coloured maybe. People don't bother too much these days. Your granny won't care what you wear. Just be nice to her, yeah? Maybe get some flowers, write a little card."

There was nothing further to be gained there and Jordan drove back to Copy Lane. The press conference would be over, and he'd swerved that particular hell. It was time to put out an alert for Pat Roach though. What he had learned just now had helped to firm up the idea squirming in the back of his mind for days. Time was short, once Serious and Organised took over he would lose control of it all no matter what DCI Griffiths said. It would go down on his record as a failure. His first case full time in Copy Lane. That bothered him. It would be a lie to say it didn't. More than that he would feel he had let Julie Scott and her mother down. He would find that hard to live with.

He stopped at the canteen to grab a cup of coffee, a ham sandwich, and a bag of crisps. He checked his uniform hanging in the locker room. It would be best to take that home tonight so he could come in ready for the funeral in the morning.

By the time he arrived in the incident room, the phones had already begun to ring with feedback. He hadn't had a chance to view the footage of the appeal, but it was bringing in results, so they had managed to get across the urgency. It could have been a mistake not including the woman, but it would have delayed things and it was too late now.

John Grice raised his arm and wagged his hand in the air. When Jordan joined him, he told the caller that they were now speaking with the officer in charge.

A gruff male voice told them, "Right, those two blokes. The ones on the telly just before, they're down the town. I saw them just now at the Pier Head. I'm nearly sure it's them, but they had a woman with them. You didn't say nothing about no woman. Anyway, youse should get down there, la. If you go now, you could nab 'em."

Chapter 71

It was almost rush hour, the trip into the city from Copy Lane would take a while. He could call St Anne Street and they would have cars there, blue lights flashing, siren blaring in a few minutes. That wouldn't work. Pat Roach and her cronies would be long gone by the time they got there.

Although he loved the Gerry Marsden landing stage and trips on the ferry, Jordan was only vaguely aware of the other sailings from the Port of Liverpool. He knew there were container boats, the occasional cruise liner, and now and again a navy ship, but his knowledge was scant.

Jordan walked to the front of the office. Just the movement was enough to grab everyone's attention. "Okay, quickly. Where can I go from the Pier Head at this time of night?"

There was a tiny hiatus and then Kath said, "The commuter ferries start at five o'clock so there's about half an hour before the first one. Then you could get over to Wallasey in ten minutes."

"There are bus stops. Could take you anywhere," Vi said. "Loads of buses."

"Yes, but you wouldn't need to go to the Pier Head for buses, there are stops all over the city," Kath said.

Jordan glanced at his watch. He should move, raise the alarm, but sending officers swarming all over the waterfront was pointless when half of them wouldn't know who they were looking for and all they would do would be to let Roach and Guthrie know they'd been seen.

Grice had been pounding on his keyboard. "Isle of Man, boss. There's a ferry in a couple of hours and one to Dublin later on."

"Surely they need a passport for Ireland? The Isle of Man wouldn't though."

"The Steam Packet Company sails from the island over to Dublin as well. If that's where they're headed. I think it's possible to do it without a passport anyway, it's part of the Common Travel Area. I'll check, but I think that's right. If they were going on anywhere after that they'd need documents, but it would give them time to maybe acquire some fakes and confuse the trail or even double-back and return to Scotland or England."

If they crossed on the Mersey ferry, they would be picked up on CCTV. He would have time to contact the police over the water and officers would be waiting for them to disembark. That wasn't his biggest worry right now. They would be picked up for sure. But he really wanted to have them now, himself. He took Stella with him and left Grice to contact Manx Ferries for a passenger list and then alert patrols in the city centre to let them know what was happening and have them stand close by in case they were needed.

The roads were busy, but if he was right, they had time. Far better to go quietly and succeed than to steam in loud and furious and scare them away. That's what his book would say was the logic behind his decision. The results would speak for themselves.

Chapter 72

They parked in Water Street in the shadow of the Liver Building. They didn't pay and their display was Jordan's police ID. The road was busy with office workers leaving for the day and commuters and trippers heading for the early ferry. Jordan and Stella joined the small flow of pedestrians heading towards the landing stage. It wasn't rushed. The boat would leave on schedule and there was always room. The breeze blowing onshore as the sun began to lower in the sky had a bit of a nip; it was pleasant by the river.

They didn't stop to lean on the railings and gaze out at the grey water of the Mersey though many people did. Everywhere phones and cameras recorded selfies and filmed videos sweeping along the riverfront and then to the Three Graces behind them. It could hold its own with any view in the world, but Jordan and Stella hadn't time to enjoy it.

"Should we split up?" Stella said.

"Not right now. We've still got a few minutes before the next ferry and if it comes to it, we can hop on board. The Steam Packet Company passenger terminal is down there. Let's give that a quick look. It's still early for that sailing. If they're in there, we'll spot them no trouble."

"No, boss, look. Over there by the railings. That's Pat Roach for sure. She's on her own."

Pat Roach was lost in her thoughts until Jordan and Stella joined her on either side and closer than was comfortable. They heard the sharp intake of breath and felt her tense.

"Just relax, Pat," Jordan said. "There's nowhere for you to go. We just want a word, and we need to speak to your two friends. We know you're all together. You were seen. Now, where are they?"

"I don't know what you're talking about. I'm just down here for a break. I've been stressed, I needed a day to myself."

"Don't lie to us anymore. It's time to just sort this out once and for all. Now, where is Richard?" Jordan said.

She turned around and took a step away from the railing. Stella placed a hand on her arm. "Keep calm, Pat. You're going to feel much better once we sort this out and you really don't have a choice anymore. It will be better for you if you help us now. Where is Richard Guthrie?"

Pat shook her head and peered off towards the ferry terminal where the evening boat was loading. Jordan leaned forward to see around her and in the distance heading towards them he saw the distinctive gait of Richard Guthrie and beside him another taller man.

Before they could react, Pat Roach raised her hand and yelled out loud across the space. Heads turned in their direction as she screamed to the two men in the distance. "Run, son. Get away. Go now."

Chapter 73

The two figures paused for a moment and then Richard Guthrie flung the drinks he had been carrying aside, and they turned and sprinted away. Stella used her Airwave set to alert the patrol cars.

Jordan left her and ran through the small crowds. He saw one of the men turn back the way he had just come to head for the Wallasey ferry. He waved his arm pointing to the walkway hoping Stella would understand what he was trying to convey.

Richard Guthrie reached The Strand with Jordan racing to catch up. He crossed the road dodging through the traffic, slapping his hands down on car bonnets. In his peripheral vision, Jordan glimpsed a patrol car, blue lights flashing, and he heard the scream of the siren among the screech of brakes and shouts of pedestrians.

Guthrie ploughed on. Jordan expected him to run down the streets into the city centre, but instead, he veered right and raced along a side turn.

The mayhem was instant. Richard Guthrie ran through the oncoming traffic and into the exit of the Queensway Tunnel. There was a cacophony of horns and scream of tyres.

It made no sense. Unless he was running blindly in his desperation to get away, he had to have known this was the wrong way to go. He might have thought he could turn at the junction inside and leave the tunnel by the other exit into the city, but no way he could make it all the way to the other side of the river. Surely, it was panic that took him into the dimness of the tunnel entrance. The only real escape was to turn and run back out. In the event, he didn't reappear. The scream of metal tearing against metal, the blaring horns and the sound of shattering glass told the story. The only question now was how many were injured in the crashed cars and what had happened to Richard Guthrie.

Jordan stopped on the narrow walkway just outside the entrance as a vehicle from the tunnel police screeched to a halt alongside. He held up his warrant card. "Stay there, mate, don't go in. There's no point right now. Let us get this sorted. We're closing the tunnel at all entrances. The emergency services are on the way. There's nothing you can do, and if meladdo managed to avoid the smash, we'll have him; we're monitoring the cameras."

As the injured were brought out, Jordan peered into the backs of the ambulances. Stella had joined him now.

"Pat Roach is on her way to Copy Lane," she said. "They've stopped anyone getting off the ferry at the other side and they've got our picture of the other bloke. I reckon they'll get him. What's happened to Guthrie?"

"He's not been brought out yet. This is not as bad as it could have been. Traffic was slowing to leave and there's a speed limit anyway. There are a few cuts and bruises. One bloke has a broken arm. Nothing too terrible. But they haven't found Richard yet. The tunnel is monitored all the way, so if he is trying to get through on foot, they'll see him. There were two cars, a motorbike, and a tourist coach in the crash but up to now nobody knows where he ended up."

They moved aside as a stretcher was wheeled past. The patient was a woman, her long hair clotted with blood. Though she was immobilised on a board and wearing a cervical collar, she was conscious and talking and the paramedic held up a thumb to Jordan.

The sergeant from the tunnel police, who had been the first into the chaos, followed the stretcher out. He came and stood in front of Jordan and Stella. He didn't need to speak, but of course he had to.

"Sorry, mate. There's nothing we can do. He's gone under the coach. He's not coming out breathing. We have to wait now for the investigation team. What the hell was he thinking?"

Once he had been in the tunnel to see Guthrie's body, there was no point waiting for him to be brought out. The CCTV cameras would show what had happened, and although reports would need to be filed, Jordan could contribute nothing useful to the proceedings right then.

"Are you okay, boss? Do you want me to drive?" Stella said.

"No, it's okay. I'm high on adrenaline at the moment I reckon, and concentrating on the traffic will calm me down. Maybe."

"This isn't what we expected, is it?"

"No, it bloody isn't. Did you get much chance to speak to Pat Roach?"

"Not really, once the shit hit the fan, I handed her over to a mobile patrol. They've taken her back to Aintree. I've messaged John to alert him and asked him to put her in an interview room."

"Good enough. When she saw them, bringing the drinks, and yelled out to them, she called him son, didn't she?"

"If it was Guthrie she meant, yes. He was the one who reacted more quickly, so I assumed it was him. It's not that unusual for people to call younger men son, though, is it?"

"No, but that doesn't feel right. Why not be specific, say, Richard or on the other hand just 'run'? We know she has a son, don't we? She told us she doesn't speak to him, but I think we know that we can't trust a word out of her mouth."

"This is going to be an interesting chat," Stella said.

Chapter 74

Somebody had provided Pat Roach with a cup of tea. She had a silver survival blanket around her shoulders. Her face was tear-streaked and she was shaking. She gripped the fragile paper cup tightly in both hands. Immediately Jordan and Stella walked into the room she yelled at them.

"Is he alright? Have you got him? I want to see him."

Although it was obvious who she meant, they had to stick to the routine. Jordan told her that she was going to be questioned under caution and he went through the rigmarole of setting up the recording equipment and identifying himself. Stella spoke to give her name and rank.

"For Christ's sake. Is he alright?" Pat said again. "Stop all this messing, tell me he's okay and where he is."

"Who are you asking about?" Jordan said.

"You know all too well. Where's my boy?"

The comment cleared up many of the questions and Jordan readjusted his approach. They had already been given the name of the other man who was on his way from Wallasey. They would use the Runcorn bridge to avoid the traffic snarl up at the tunnel.

He knew the answer, but the question had to be asked. "Do you mean Richard Carl Guthrie? Or are you referring to Stephen Storey?"

"You know bloody well. I saw Stephen. He got on the ferry. I suppose you've stopped him. I want to know about Rich. Where is he, what happened?"

There was no easy way to do this. Jordan knew straightforward and simple was best. "I'm sorry, Pat, Richard was involved in a traffic accident. He didn't survive. They are looking after him and you will be able to see him in due course."

Pat stared at him open-mouthed for a few beats and then her face crumpled, the cup of cold tea dropped from her hand spilling across the table. She curled forward, wrapping her arms around her body; the silver blanket slid to the floor with a quiet shushing noise.

"I am sorry, Pat. Do you need some time?" Stella said, but the only response was a groan of despair followed by quiet sobbing.

They left the interview room and Jordan arranged for the duty nurse to attend to Pat. "Nothing we can do until she gets herself together," he said. "Have we an ETA for this other bloke?"

"I'll find out," Stella said. "I shouldn't be long."

Chapter 75

Stephen Storey was handcuffed, and two uniformed officers had been stationed at the door to the interview room. The one outside leaned to open the door and let them in. "He's pretty wound up, sir. Put up a bit of a fight when they stopped him on the ferry. We've already got him for assaulting a police officer."

"Has he asked for a solicitor?" Jordan said.

"No, though he was offered one. He's been given a drink and isn't injured in any way."

Jordan introduced himself and Stella, asked again if the prisoner wanted legal representation and set up the recording. "Where's my mate and his mum?"

"Who do you mean?"

"You know bloody well. Just don't be messin' with me here, chum."

"I'm sorry but I need to tell you that Richard Guthrie has been in an accident."

"Shit, that's on you that is. You chased him for no reason. I saw you. Is he okay?"

"I'm afraid not, no."

"What did you have to do that for? Why did you have to scare him like that? What have we done? We haven't done nothing."

"So why did you run?"

"Well, anybody would. Pat was yelling and then you started running, anybody would have reacted like that."

"Only if they had something to hide," Stella said.

"Not me, not us. We've got nothing to hide."

Jordan showed Storey the picture of him in the car with Richard Guthrie. "That's you."

Stephen leaned forward to look more closely. "Might be."

"What can you tell me about that car?"

"It's a Ford."

"Oh, very funny. Who owns it?"

"Not me."

"And yet you are riding around in it."

"Yeah well, that's what they're for, innit."

"Was it Richard's?"

"Dunno. You'd need to ask him."

"We can't do that," Stella said.

"Why?"

"I'm afraid Mr Guthrie didn't survive the accident."

"Aw, no. Rich. Dead? You're lying. He's not, is he? He's not really?"

"I'm afraid so. It's probably time for you to tell us just what's been going on so we can find out who is responsible for what. If not, we'll have to assume that you were equally involved, and we're investigating a very serious crime."

They expected him to ask for a lawyer, but either the shock of hearing about his friend had knocked the wind out of his sails or he had seen a way to turn it to his advantage. His eyes were wet, and he shook his head.

"You're talking about that geek, aren't you? It was an accident. All we wanted to do was scare the bloke. We wanted something he had, and he was being a dick about it. Rich started to knock him about a bit, and it went too far. I tried to stop it, I did, but he slipped. He cracked his head on the window ledge. He was bleeding pretty bad, so we got scared and left."

"Not too scared to take his security system and to go to his shop and take things away with you. You should have helped him."

"Yes, I know, but it was all mad; out of control. That was Rich. He said the main thing was the computer, it was his mam's. It was a laptop and she needed it back and it was important. But the bloke was a pillock. Rich said there was something off about it all."

Jordan decided it might be best to appear to believe him. "Okay. So, was Richard close to his mum?"

"Pretty close, I'd say. They used to meet up a bit. Rich has a flat in Spain, and his mum would go out there to stay with him. I never went."

"Why's that?"

"Never fancied it. I like it here. I'm English, I am. I haven't even got a passport."

"So, did they meet up in England then?"

"Now and again. Look, I don't know much about her. I've known Rich for a bit. We were close, but I only met her a couple of times. She wanted this laptop, said it was important and there was some money in it for us if we got it."

"Where is it now?"

"I don't know. Rich had it, and he was going to get it back to her. He said he had to wait a bit until things had calmed down. I don't know what things."

"What do you know about Julie Scott?" Jordan said.

The other man shook his head. "Never heard of her; who's that?"

Jordan showed him the personnel photograph. "Nah. Never seen her, have I?"

"You never went to her house at Old Roan?"

"Don't remember doing that; no, like I said, never seen her. Listen, mate, I'm tired, I've had a horrible shock, my mucka's dead and I don't feel well. I can't do no more today. You need to speak to Rich's mum, that's what all this has been about. Some laptop. That's all I know. I think I need to have a solicitor because you're doing my head in and I'm finished with this."

Chapter 76

Pat Roach looked diminished. She was crumpled and grubby. The nurse had declared her fit for questioning on the condition that if she became distressed, they would call for a medical opinion.

"You might as well just tell us everything you know," Jordan said quietly.

She looked across the table with watery eyes and sniffed.

"It was all my fault. Richard's a good boy... was a good boy. He was helping me. I needed him to fetch something for me and it all went wrong."

"The laptop," Jordan said.

"Oh. So, you know. Was it that Stephen who told you? I never liked him much, but Richard was fond of him, and they'd been mates for a long time. Mind, he's been quick enough to flap his trap, hasn't he, Stephen? Anyway, the bloke wouldn't give them the computer and they had a fight. It was accidental. Richard was cut up about it, especially when we heard the bloke had died. He panicked and turned up at mine, said we had to get away."

They told her they had already worked out what was going on and just needed confirmation and she might as well make it quick and as easy as possible. They told her what they had surmised had happened between herself and Julie.

"Why were you really friends with her, Pat? You didn't have anything much in common. Was it all contrived because of what she knew?" Jordan asked.

Pat took a breath and seemed to settle her mind.

"It was like I told you. At first, it was just chance. I'd worked at plenty of places, and when the vacancy came up at Harding and Harding, I couldn't believe it. I already knew she worked there, and I really did want to get her and Paul back together. Then we got closer. Okay, I sort of made it happen but anyway, she started to confide. She had this big problem – that's what she said. She was going to confront her boss. The idea was to get him to bring it all out in the open. For him to confess what he was doing and hand himself over to you lot. She was stupid and couldn't see what a chance she was missing."

"She was scared," she continued, "that was all. But I was talking her round. I got her to go with me to Spain. I was going to get Rich to go and get the laptop and once I had it, I'd have the upper hand. But then she put the laptop in the shop. For safety, she said. She told the bloke she wanted some new software on and didn't know how to do it. She was away with the fairies. How was that safe, giving the thing to someone else who could root around inside? She said it was in hidden folders. Might have been. I don't know. She was better at that stuff than I was. She showed me the receipt, I had the chance and so I took it. She never knew. There was no need for Richard then. Paul was supposed to go and get the thing back while we were away. It was going to be much better if I had it. I could take her problem away, couldn't I? Really make proper use of it, and she'd go along once she saw how much we could make. The way I look at it, he was a crook anyway, so why not make him pay? We could have gone on for ages, and in the end, we could dob him in. We couldn't lose. But Paul cocked up, he lost the receipt."

"So, what happened with Richard? Why kill her? What was the sense in that?" Jordan asked. "We are waiting for DNA results from the scene. We already have his on record. I don't think there is going to be any way out of this. He's dead, Pat. At least there won't be the pain of a trial and seeing him in jail for years and years. I realise that's no comfort, but there's no sense in lying about it either. You might as well just tell us what happened."

"He didn't. He went to her house while we were away. When I was giving her a hard time about the laptop, she said she had a backup of the information anyway. We were thinking files or a folder – hard copy. But he mistimed it, and she nearly caught him, and he ran away. That's all he did. Okay, he smashed the place up. I didn't like that and then she nearly caught him. He said he wanted to make it look like an ordinary robbery."

"He was seen by someone else leaving over the back wall," Stella said.

Now Pat began to cry. Tears streamed down her face, and she sniffed and wiped them away with the heel of her hand.

"But that was later? He was trying to help me. He went back to help me. Oh God, this is all my fault, and my boy is dead because of me."

Chapter 77

They had to call a halt. If Pat Roach was found to have been too distressed to be questioned, a defence lawyer would make much of it. Back in the incident room, Grice, Stella, and Jordan ate bacon rolls from the canteen, drank black coffee, and threw around ideas.

It was understandable, they agreed, that she wouldn't admit that her son had killed Julie. But he was already guilty of manslaughter according to Stephen's statement. He was dead and his memory was forever besmirched. Paul Palmer would have to answer for his part in it, but he hadn't done much. There were the dolls, but that was little more than a prank, a nuisance at the most. As for everything else, it could be argued that since he hadn't used the original receipt, he hadn't done anything.

"What's the situation with the DNA?" Jordan asked.

"I've tried to put a rush on it, but it takes however long it takes. Could be a few days yet," Grice said.

"I guess we'll just have to wait then. I suppose it's fairly academic, but we do need to draw a line under it. Have we got enough to hold Pat?" Stella said.

"The trouble is that she didn't do that much either, as far as we know. She nicked a receipt and she tried to talk Julie into blackmail, but even that never happened. If we find the laptop now, which is what I expect when we go through Guthrie's stuff, wherever that is, it'll just be passed to St Anne Street. It'll make their job easier, but it won't do much for us. If Stephen Storey sticks to his account, we can try and have him for his part in the death of poor Joe. We'll need to prove that he could have foreseen that there'd be a fight or he took part in it – that might be tricky. Richard Guthrie is dead, and Julie is dead and we're going to have to depend on the scant evidence we have and DNA to prove anything. We already know that he was in the house, so of course he's left traces. I think we have problems here, boss." Grice gathered up the takeaway containers and logged out of his computer. "I'm banjaxed, and you two must be absolutely shattered. How about we call it a day? Pat Roach is going to be released pending further investigation. I don't think she'll make a run for it. Not with her boy in the morgue. I'd suggest we have another look after the funeral tomorrow with fresh minds."

"Okay, sounds like a plan," Jordan said. "Why don't we meet up at Doris's house. The hearse is going past there, and it would be nice to give her a bit of support, I think it's at eleven so maybe meet at ten fifteen in Old Roan."

He watched them leave and then turned back to his computer.

Chapter 78

It was a grey, dismal day. Doris Beetham's house was busy with neighbours and colleagues of Julie's. No one quite knew what they should do, and there wasn't enough room for everyone to sit. Doris was in a chair beside the fire, frail and dignified, though her eyes were red-rimmed and watery.

There was a lull when Jordan, Stella and Grice arrived. Jordan had been late home and his eyes looked heavy, but he was an imposing figure in uniform.

A few of the younger people glared, and there was a comment about them turning up when it was too late. For once Jordan didn't blame them. Going through the files again proved that there was probably no way anyone could have predicted the horrible outcome, but that was little comfort.

Pat Roach wasn't there, but a patrol car had confirmed that there had been lights on in the house most of the night and the curtains had been drawn back in the morning. She had made an appointment to visit the morgue later in the day to see her son and Jordan wasn't concerned that she would run. He expected her to turn up at the cemetery.

The hearse drew up outside. Mourners stood aside to allow Doris, leaning on the arm of the woman from next door, to walk out. She paused for a moment to view the coffin and the flowers and then slid into the limousine waiting behind.

The cemetery was huge, and even as they arrived there were cars from an earlier funeral leaving. As *Amazing Grace* began to play through speakers in the chapel, the coffin and principal mourners filed in past pews filled with the sad, the dutiful, and the inquisitive. There was no religious service, just a humanist address delivered by an elderly celebrant who did his best with what had to have been little knowledge of Julie. He referenced her sudden and shocking passing and Jordan was aware of eyes on them where they sat near the back of the place. After what seemed too short a time to record the end of a life, the strains of *Somewhere over the Rainbow* began, and they left. Doris thanked them for coming and asked them back to the house. Jordan had spotted Pat in the hubbub around the door and at his nod Stella had moved close.

"We can't come back now, Mrs Beetham," he said, "but we'll call in to see you in a couple of days."

"I'm glad you got him. I wish he'd had to answer for what he did to my girl, but then we can't have everything, can we?"

Jordan didn't respond. He shook the dry, bony hand and turned to where Grice had joined Stella, with Pat Roach between them.

She knew. Her face was set and her chin up, but she knew just what was about to happen. There was the flicker of panic, quickly controlled. "Don't do it here, not in front of all these."

Jordan spoke quietly to recite the caution. They didn't put handcuffs on her, but a patrol car was parked behind the chapel building waiting to transport her back to Copy Lane.

* * *

The fight had gone out of Pat Roach. Her son was gone, and she didn't have the heart to struggle any longer. She shook her head and began to speak in a low monotone.

"I never meant for this to happen. She wouldn't give me the receipt or the backup records she had. Said she'd changed her mind. Too upset about what had happened with the robbery and the dolls, and it was karma, silly bitch. We argued. I tried to make her see sense. She was tidying and putting stuff in boxes to give away. She wouldn't even listen. She had her phone and threatened to call him right then and tell him what she knew. We struggled because that was just stupid. It just happened. One minute she was waving the phone around and yelling at me to go away and leave her alone. I tried to stop her faffing about and listen to me. I should never have picked up the knife. I only meant to scare her. She was using it to cut tape. Why not use scissors? If she'd used scissors, it wouldn't have happened. It was just lying there on the table. You see she just wouldn't listen. All I wanted was for her to see the sense of it. It was an accident really." Pat was shivering now and gulping back tears.

"But you didn't call for help?" Stella said.

"There was no point. She was dead, I could tell. Then I thought if I could get the laptop, I could sell it to her boss at Hardings. He'd pay well for that, wouldn't he? All I needed was the receipt. If I had money, I could go. Me and Rich, we could have made a new start. I never had nothing, I didn't give up my baby until there was no choice. I tried my best as long as I could. I even gave him his dad's name, so he didn't get bullied, so he never got called Cock Roach, not like me. I tried for as long as I could, and I always knew where he was. Not her, she'd turned her back on her boy. He was a nice little lad. That's not right. She was selfish. I reckoned it was my turn. I tried to help her, and I did try to stop the blood, but then she stopped breathing. She could just have given me the papers. I didn't know where to look and I had to get away, I had to get rid of her phone and the knife and that horrible cloth, all bloody."

She began to cry now and hid behind her hands. Mourners were staring as they passed on their way to the cars.

"There were no papers," Stella said.

"But she said. Backup copies, she said."

"Yes, but they were on her Kindle."

"Don't be so bloody daft. It wasn't a book."

There was no point in trying to explain and they had what they needed. St Anne Street had enough to pursue the fraudsters at Harding and Harding. With a confession, they would put Pat Roach away for a long time. If she had called for help, it might have gone easier for her, but she hadn't, and the greed and the lying had made things much worse.

It was possible that nobody would really pay for the death of Joe Brady who had simply been doing his job and indulging in what he enjoyed. A good defence lawyer would point to the lack of evidence against Stephen Storey who had admitted being in the house, but denied having any part in the fight that killed the geek. It was up to the CPS to make the hard decisions there.

The patrol car drove slowly down the long drive as Doris Beetham climbed into her limousine. Grice turned to Jordan. "What was it, boss? I thought we'd covered everything."

"Just one of those niggles at the back of my mind. It was all about timing. When we mentioned that Richard was seen leaving over the wall, she knew that it was later, after the murder. If he had done it, she would have assumed that was what we meant. She knew he couldn't have been seen leaving if he wasn't there, but she was."

It was a sad and messy case and there would always be the frisson of guilt that they hadn't prevented the murder of Julie Scott. There would be an internal inquiry. It was already supposed that no blame would be apportioned, but Jordan knew it would sit with him for the rest of his life. He always remembered victims, but this one would cause him more grief than most.

The End

List of characters

Detective Inspector Jordan Carr – Jamaican heritage. Married to Penny. They have one baby – Harry.

Lizzie – Penny's sister.

DS Stella May – Liverpool born and bred. Lives in Aintree.

Nana Gloria – Jordan's granny.

David Griffiths – Detective Chief Inspector with Serious and Organised Crime.

John Grice – Newly promoted detective.

Stephen (Steve) – Works in the digital forensics department.

DCI Josh Lewis – In charge at Copy Lane.

Kath Webster and Violet Purcell – Junior officers.

Karen – Josh Lewis's secretary.

Ted Bliss – Crime scene sergeant.

Sergeant Flowers – CSI acerbic, and a bit sarcastic.

Dr James Jasper – Medical examiner based at the University of Liverpool.

DS Mark Bolland – Based in Blackpool. Misogynist, racist and thoroughly unpleasant.

Sue – Technician based in Blackpool.

If you enjoyed this book, please let others know by leaving a quick review on Amazon. Also, if you spot anything untoward in the paperback, get in touch. We strive for the best quality and appreciate reader feedback.

editor@thebookfolks.com

www.thebookfolks.com

Other titles of interest

THE PIPER'S CHILDREN by Iain Henn

The first standalone book in a new series of mysteries set in the US

A boy is found wandering in the woods, dressed in medieval clothes and speaking a strange language. When another child turns up, it doesn't shed any more light on the mystery for FBI agent Ilona Farris. Only by digging into her own past will she begin to work out what is going on, and who these children are, seemingly lost in time.

YOUR COLD EYES by Denver Murphy

A standalone serial killer thriller set in the UK

A serial killer is targeting women. He is dressing them up and discarding their bodies. Detectives become convinced that it is something about the way the victims look that is making them be selected. They need to find out just what that is, and why, to hunt down the killer.

Printed in Great Britain
by Amazon

35136563R00126